Beyond Death
(The Afterlife Series Book 1)
By Deb McEwan

The right of Deb McEwan to be identified as the author of this work has been asserted by her in accordance with the Copyright, Designs and Patents Act 1988.

This is a work of fiction. While some places and events are a matter of fact, the characters are the product of the author's imagination and are used in a fictitious manner. Any resemblance to actual persons, living or dead, is purely coincidental.

Cover Design by Jessica Bell

Chapter 1

It shouldn't have happened; it wasn't her time. But they were busy and weren't paying attention, so she died.

*****

Ken parked outside Big Ed's shop and waited. He could see the three girls through the window, two playing on the fruit machines and the other waiting with a look on her face that screamed an attitude only teenagers were capable of displaying. He saw the door open at the back of the shop and the good-looking big man appeared from behind the counter. He said something to the girls and waited for the two to finish playing. They obviously thought they were calling the shots but Ken knew differently. A few minutes later they approached the car.

'All right, Ken?' asked Big Ed and Ken nodded. He looked at the man's tattooed arms and biceps bulging out of his t-shirt, and his chest that was on a par with the average silver back. Ken smiled and nodded again. Even if he wasn't *all right* he wouldn't argue with this man.

'Usual place, Ed?' Big Ed nodded and hustled the girls into the back seat.

'Come on girls. You're going to love this party.'

About halfway there Ken had switched off to the chatter and giggles of the two girls. The third seemed to be unusually quiet and as he wondered why, she spoke.

'Stop the car please. I want to get out.'

Ken looked at Big Ed in the mirror and he gave a little shake of his head so he carried on driving.

The girl wasn't happy she'd been ignored. 'Stop the car now!' she said, taking her phone out of her pocket. 'I'll call someone if you don't let me out.'

'Okay, okay,' said Big Ed. 'Calm down, darling. Nobody's going to force you to go to a party, have lots of fun, free drink and food and drive you back so your teachers won't know where you've been,' he winked at the other two, 'instead of pretending you're visiting a friend's house and doing your homework.'

The other girls sniggered and Mel wondered if she was doing the right thing by not going.

'Come on, Mel,' said one of her friends, 'we won't get caught so don't be such a nerd.'

Never one to go with the flow, Mel was feeling uneasy about the outing and decided to trust her gut instinct. 'I've changed my mind. Let me out.'

Big Ed didn't like the look of this one and thought she could be trouble. All the other girls had been compliant until getting there at the very least. He'd had a bit of trouble from one or two after the initial visit but had soon put them in the picture. He'd totally bent the returners to his will and put the fear of the devil in the one that had refused to return. After a little slapping and a few threats, he was confident she'd keep her mouth shut. It was a shame about this one, though as she was a proper looker but he decided to cut his losses. He put on his most charming smile.

'What about you girls? Are you going with Mel or staying with me?'

'You're having a laugh, Ed aren't you?' said Drew as she squeezed his thigh and gave him a seductive smile, 'I wouldn't miss this party for the world.'

'Free booze and partying on a school night. Are you mad, Mel?' said Alice as she wondered what planet her friend was on.

Big Ed indicated for Ken to pull up to the kerb and Mel tried to give her friends a warning look before getting out of the car but they chose to ignore her. Her dad had always said that you don't get anything for nothing and she wondered what her friends would have to do in return for the free booze and other stuff. She hoped her father was right otherwise she'd be mad she'd missed a good party.

Ken watched the youngster cross the road and head for the bus stop. He could tell she'd turn into a right one when she was older and no doubt give some poor mug the run around. It would never happen to him though and he was looking forward to seeing Val later on. Uncomplicated sex then send her back home. Her unsuspecting husband would be none the wiser because she'd still be asleep when he came home off night shift. Ken didn't feel guilty about putting his mate on nights; he'd send Val back to him when he got bored with her and good old Ron would be none the wiser.

Mel took the bus back to the stop near Alice's house. Alice's parents were working and she walked round the back to retrieve the key from underneath the plant pot, letting herself in the back door after checking that no one was looking. Their school uniforms were hanging in Alice's wardrobe. Mel changed and removed her make up before making her way back into school without anyone knowing she'd been further than her friend's. They had the excuse of going to Alice's to do their homework. Alice was spoilt rotten and her parents would cover for her, no matter the situation. They were happy for her to go to boarding school so they didn't have to take time out from their busy jobs during the week and Alice was happy to spend time with her friends and get up to so much that her parents didn't have a clue about.

*****

3

Enjoying some down time between shifts Ken was in his underpants and had been looking out of his bedroom window into the garden next door for a little while. The line was half-full and Mrs Wallace was hobbling around touching items, checking how dry they were, Ken assumed. She rubbed her hands on her old-fashioned pinafore and picked up her basket as she slowly made her way back towards her kitchen door. Before she reached it she stopped and looked skyward. Ken noticed the spots on the pathway and before long they were all joined together. He laughed as the widow hobbled as fast as she could back to the washing line, trying in vain to stop the clothes and bedding from getting wet. She was as wet as her washing by the time she struggled back into her house with an overflowing basket. Stupid old woman. He laughed out loud and turned as he heard the bedroom door open.

Ken felt a jolt in his gut when he looked at her. She wasn't stunningly beautiful but had something about her and if he'd been the type to hook up with a woman, this is the one he would have chosen. He crossed the room and grabbed her roughly. Loosening her dressing gown, he grabbed one of her nipples and gave it a squeeze.

'Come on then, Val let's have some dinner. Ken's hungry, and maybe after,' he smacked her behind, 'we'll go again and have some more fun.'

Val looked at the man she'd been seeing behind her husband's back and realisation dawned. He wasn't a good person on the inside or out and she felt shame and guilt. She did love her husband but they'd taken each other for granted and were drifting apart. She'd fallen for Ken when he'd paid her attention at a time she was feeling particularly unloved and unwanted. Val now realised she didn't want the deceit and lies anymore. She still loved Ron and wanted to save her marriage. The sooner this stupid affair was

4

over the better. 'I'm not staying for dinner, Ken. It's been a huge mistake and it's over.' It was almost a whisper but shocking in its intensity. He hadn't expected it and looked totally bewildered. For once he didn't have a smart arse comment and Val felt a little sorry for him.

'Look, Ken. I love Ron and want our marriage to work.'

'I'm going to tell him what you've done,' said Ken, obviously smarting from her comments. Val wasn't in the mood for an argument. She knew he'd never confront her husband. She also knew that he'd soon find another weak, vulnerable woman to share his bed.

'You know you won't do that,' she said, getting dressed. 'I'll get my stuff together and leave and we can forget this ever happened.'

'But, Val. I don't want to...'

Decision made, she went to the bathroom to collect her belongings and closed the door, not wishing to hear any more. She leant against it for a couple of seconds taking a few deep breaths. Val could hear him banging about the bedroom. She splashed cold water onto her face and left the tap running to blot out some of the noise coming from the bedroom. She knew he had a temper so decided to take her time and give him a chance to calm down a bit. It hadn't been pleasant but Val felt calm and in control again. Hopefully she could make it up to Ron. Despite his shortcomings he didn't deserve to be deceived by his wife and so called best mate. She gave it a few more minutes, double-checked that she'd collected all her toiletries and other paraphernalia, and psyched herself up for departure. Determined not to get into an argument or discussion Val took a deep breath then opened the en-suite door to enter the bedroom. The scene before her took her breath away and Val yelped. She put her hand over her

5

open mouth and chewed on the fleshy part of her palm, trying to control the panic that was welling up inside.

'Ken! Ken!'

He was half-lying on the floor and leaning against the bed, the quilt at his side. Val shook him but his body slumped fully onto the floor. Trying to remember what to do, Val vaguely recalled seeing adverts about how to resuscitate heart attack victims. Shaking, she laid him flat and held his nose while trying to breathe air into his lungs, the *Stayin' Alive* song on repeat in her head. No reaction so Val kneeled over him and started the chess presses. After ten minutes of trying both, she sat back exhausted.

'Oh My God. Oh My God,' she muttered to no one in particular. She reached for her mobile changed her mind and picked up Ken's phone instead and dialled nine, nine, nine.

'Ambulance please.'

The operator had to concentrate to understand the caller who sounded as if she had a speech impediment. She made a note of the address and the caller's name, Jane Smith, before the caller hung up. Val put on a pair of gloves and got a cloth from the kitchen. Feeling like a criminal she wiped all the surfaces she thought might contain her fingertips then dressed quickly. She checked to make sure she hadn't forgotten anything and left the flat as quietly as she could, convinced her heart would burst out of her chest. It was drizzling and windy and the street was deserted. She decided to walk home. Although she hadn't committed any crime she felt frightened and guilty and didn't want to be seen. It was a relatively safe neighbourhood so she hoped the walk would calm her and enable her to collect her thoughts.

*****

Ken thought he was having a nightmare. He felt fingers prodding him and he couldn't breathe. The

6

fingers turned to fully formed hands and they multiplied as he watched in fascination as their prodding became more urgent and they started to pull and poke his body. It took him a while to realise he wasn't sleeping.

The cold realisation that the pain in his chest had killed him hit like a punch in the guts. He would have been furious had he not been so frightened. Ken tried to compose himself and wait for the beckoning white light that he knew must surely come. But the scabby, gnarled and bloody hands started dragging him downwards. To add to his fear, he looked around and saw a number of faces closing in, some tortuous, some with cruel smiles, but all gruesome. The hands pulled him further down and the faces taunted him.

He screamed but no one came to help.

*****

Claire stormed into the living room to confront Tash.

'Right, what's going on?'

Used to her best friend's drama queen outbursts, Tash didn't take her eyes off the telly.

'Don't know what you're on about, Claire,' she said.

Claire turned off the TV and went to stand right in front of her.

'Now I've got your attention, I need to know what's going on. Jay's been acting funny for the last week or so and you...' Claire frowned as Tash smiled innocently. 'See, that's what I mean. You're all sweetness and light and smugness,' said Claire, 'and I've heard the whispering in the office stop whenever I walk into a room. It's making me paranoid.'

Tash folded her arms and continued smiling and Claire could see that her current tactics were getting her nowhere. She decided to appeal to her best friend's better side.

'Please, Tash. Tell me what's going on. Jay's not going to dump me is he?'

Claire knew very well that Jay was as mad about her as she was about him and no way was he going to dump her. She also knew this was unfair but could see Tash waiver. Tash was still recovering from her last relationship, which had ended a few months previously when she'd discovered that the love of her life had also called two other women the love of his life. As Claire suspected, this did the trick.

'What date is it?'

'5th of August,' Claire replied and Tash raised her eyebrows.

'The second anniversary of when we met, of course I haven't forgotten. Ah.'

The penny dropped.

'So he's doing a special dinner or something to celebrate our anniversary tonight, even though it's a work day tomorrow?' She took a moment, trying to work it all out and her best friend decided to put her out of her misery, even though she'd promised Jay she'd keep his secret. What the hell, she'd already told half the office staff.

'You can be extremely stupid at times, Claire, even by your standards. Jay wants to make your second anniversary even more special by proposing to you, you Muppet!'

Claire fell onto the sofa, shocked into silence. A smile spread slowly across her face and she jumped up and started skipping around the room, clapping her hands and laughing. Tash shook her head. She was over the moon for her but regretted her own indiscretion. She also regretted telling the girls at work but Claire was her current priority. She'd done so well keeping the truth from her for this long and she'd fallen at the last hurdle. Now she had to convince her to act as if she knew nothing.

Tash waited for the initial euphoria to wear off and Claire sat down next to her, still giggling and breathless.

'I take it you're going to say yes then?' and Claire nodded.

'The thing is, I promised Jay that I'd keep it a secret so you're going to have to act as if it's a complete surprise otherwise you'll spoil all his preparations.'

'I can do that,' said Claire, 'but why did he need to tell you?'

Tash knew what was coming and decided to be patient. She hoped Claire didn't suspect anything; she still felt guilty even though it had happened ages ago.

'Tash?'

Tash returned to the present. 'Simple, Claire. Jay wanted to prepare a special menu full of your favourites. He knows that you change your mind about what you like almost on a daily basis so he told me so he could keep up-to-date and make it soooo special.'

She could see Claire wasn't totally convinced so carried on.

'He wants to make this evening really special for you so he asked for my help. You know what a brill cook and a perfectionist he is and he wanted everything to be perfect. You're having orange and melon for starters, your favourite chicken for main and some sort of strawberry and chocolate concoction for dessert.'

'I would have preferred one of his legendary soups for starters.' Claire tried to keep a straight face.

'You ungrateful...'

'Got you. Only joking,' she clapped and laughed. They were always trying to wind each other up and Claire was pleased to have got one over on Tash. She put her minor triumph to one side and turned serious.

'You guys have gone to all this trouble for me?' Before she answered, Claire hugged her friend and flatmate, silently thanking the gods of fate for her lovely friends and family, but mostly for sending Jay her way.

They stopped hugging and Claire held her at arm's length. 'I promise I won't let on until we've been married for a few years and we can all have a good laugh about it then.' Both girls had tears in their eyes and Claire got up from the sofa, wiping hers away.

'I'm going to ruin my mascara if I'm not careful,' she said, running to the bathroom. She went to her room after leaving the bathroom and stared at her reflection in the dressing table mirror. Her chat with Tash and the fact that she'd worked late meant she didn't have enough time to sort herself out. She hastily put on another coat of mascara and pinned back her fringe with a slide. She usually straightened her fringe and let the rest of her hair do its own thing. Jay loved her curls and whenever she told him her hair was driving her nuts he ran his fingers through it and said that was beautiful.

'Love is blind,' she said out loud and smiled at her reflection, knowing she looked good in her skinny jeans and bustier top. She grabbed her bag and shouted goodbye to her flatmate.

'I won't expect to see you later tonight then.'

Claire popped her head around the door and hurriedly said that she'd be back but probably early in the morning as usual for a Friday. It was so much easier in the rush hour to get to work from their flat instead of Jay's and she often took a taxi home early morning and showered at her own place before leaving for work.

'I can't afford to take another sickie and I need to save my days off for Christmas, so I'll definitely be back. Anyway, if I took extra stuff with me on a Thursday, Jay would know the secret was out,' she shouted before leaving.

Fair point agreed Tash as she watched her friend disappear through the front door, unaware that this would be the last conversation they'd ever have.

*****

Claire left the train 50 minutes later and made her way out of the station. She usually ignored everyone and everything on the ten-minute walk to Jay's flat but this evening she wanted to share her happiness and smiled at everyone and everything. She looked around her. Nature seemed to be putting on a special private show just for her and she listened to the birdsong and looked at the beautiful flowers as she passed gardens. Her senses seemed to be heightened and she stopped to look at bees buzzing around lavender bushes at the border of the park. She sniffed and the scent reminded her of her late grandmother's garden. If it hadn't been for the money left to her by her grandmother she wouldn't have been able to afford to move to London and train as a Legal Secretary. Although the company was sponsoring her it had still been a big step to move from her home and retail job to the capital. Her twin brothers had helped her find a place and had introduced her to Tash, who worked for the same company as Jim and had advertised for a flatmate. If she hadn't made the move she would never have met Jay. Claire looked up to the late summer sky and muttered a thank you, imagining her grandmother could hear her – she wanted to thank everyone this evening. A few youngsters playing football in the park stopped to look at the mad woman who was talking to the sky and Claire laughed self-consciously and carried on her way, thoughts turning to her future. Her evening classes would be completed the following month and her five-year plan was to get promoted within the next year and to start a family when they'd been married for about a year. She would like two or three children

11

within that five-year period but knew that Jay wasn't a lover of big families. She was sure she could get him to see things her way and continued smiling to herself as she reached the house. She looked up at it before approaching the door. Jay's flat on the third floor wouldn't be big enough when they married, especially when they started a family, so they would need to move. It should be sooner rather than later thought Claire, because she wanted to stamp her individuality on their own place wherever that might be. She knew she was getting ahead of herself so tried to contain her excitement. Plenty of time for that later she thought as she pressed the buzzer.

'Who is it?' he said over the intercom and Claire loved the fact that his voice quickened her pulse still, even after two years together.

'It's me and I've forgotten my key again. Sorry.'

She heard him laughing and the click signalled he'd unlocked the outer door. She entered and walked up the stairs, composing herself so that she didn't give anything away.

It was pretty obvious something was going on as soon as she entered the flat. Even though it was still light outside there were candles throughout the lounge and Jay had opened out the small dining table and placed a lit candle in the middle. They kissed as if they hadn't seen each other for weeks not one day, then Jay handed the love of his life a glass of champagne.

'Happy anniversary, darling. This is the second of many.' They clinked glasses and Claire looked around.

'Someone's been very busy and all for our anniversary?'

He nodded and winked. 'You know you're worth it, Claire. Now go and sit down so I can spoil you.'

She looked up to the ceiling and for the third time that evening thanked her lucky stars for the day she met this man. She didn't know what she'd done to deserve this happiness and was amazed that the physical side of their relationship was still electrifying. Their love life was out of this world and made her two previous serious relationships seem like kids' stuff. She looked at Jay. The man she loved was gorgeous, kind, could cook and didn't mind doing household chores, and he adored her as well. Life was perfect.

'Okay?' Jay could see the expression on Claire's face and knew that this would be a night to remember. She smiled in reply and he put the plates on the table and nodded his head in its direction.

The orange and melon was delicious and left plenty of room for the main event.

'Shall I clean up as we go while you're sorting the main course?' she asked.

'You just stay where you are, darling I don't want you to lift a finger tonight,' he said, and Claire smiled in reply.

As he'd expected, she loved the main course and he pushed the plates to one side when they'd both finished. 'More champagne?'

'Don't mind if I do, babes,' she said, pushing her glass forward. He recharged both. He looked at the woman he adored and decided the time was right for the question but Claire had other plans.

'Jay, before you serve dessert I just wanted to give you this,' she bent to the floor and picked up a wrapped package. 'It's only a small anniversary present but when I saw it I knew it was exactly right for you.'

He opened the package carefully so that the paper didn't rip, and was delighted when he saw what was in the box.

'A genuine Swiss Army watch, waterproof to what…' he scanned the leaflet, 'two hundred and fifty metres. Claire, it's perfect, exactly what I've always wanted.'

The watch was tough and would be great for all his outdoor pursuits. He left the table and grabbed hold of her, picking her up and swinging her around.

'Thank you, darling. It's great.'

'Put me down I'm going to be sick.' He put her down but enveloped her in a big hug. His smile disappeared as quickly as it had arrived and, solemn faced he released her.

'Please sit down. There's something I need to say.'

Although she knew this was coming Claire felt the butterflies dance in her stomach and she started shaking. She returned to her seat and looked at her boyfriend. He took her hand.

'You know I've loved you more or less since the first time we set eyes on each other don't you?'

'What do you mean, more or less?' she said and Jay laughed, thinking it typical of her to latch on to the negative.

'Okay, it wasn't until the second date that I was one hundred per cent sure but by then I knew I wanted to spend my life with you.'

Satisfied, she didn't interrupt further.

Letting go of her hand, he knelt on the floor on one knee and produced a small box. He opened the box and smiled.

'Claire Sylvester, will you marry me?'

Claire was laughing and crying at the same time and quickly reached inside her bag for a tissue to wipe her eyes and nose.

'Yes, oh yes. Of course I will.'

Jay slid the solitaire on her finger and the ring was a perfect fit.

'Tash?' she asked and he nodded, lifting his fiancée to her feet.

They kissed, slowly and then hungrily, as if nothing else in the world existed. Dessert was forgotten as he led her to the bedroom where they made love urgently at first then leisurely the second time, savouring each and every moment and lingering over the exquisite hidden places of their bodies. Both were still awestruck at the intensity of feeling.

Exhausted and totally satiated, they slept the sleep of the dead.

*****

Ron was absolutely knackered. He'd agreed to do a month of night shifts for his mate Ken, who was also his boss. Ken had told him that he was short of reliable taxi drivers, but Ron had found it hard to believe as the recession meant that loads of people were applying for few jobs, but he'd convinced him.

'Look, mate. I know that for every vacancy we get twenty applicants but that's only because they have to apply,' Ken had said, 'not because they want to.' He went on to say that the firm might go bust and that Ron could lose his job if that happened.

'It's only for a month until we train the new guys. Then you can go back to days and the occasional night shift.'

Ron had reluctantly agreed but was having problems adjusting to his new routine and seemed to be always tired. The extra money would be handy to give Val the holiday she'd always wanted, though. She'd been distant and snappish recently and, whatever was wrong, he wanted to put it right and celebrate their 25th wedding anniversary in style. He'd spoken to Libby their oldest, and she'd agreed it was a good idea. Their son Carl didn't have a clue what was going on and Ron was happy to keep it that way.

The night had been quiet so far and Ron had snatched forty minutes sleep before the radio brought him back with a jolt.

'You there, Ron?' Sheila sounded pissed off and Ron answered straight away.

'Of course I'm here.'

'Answer your damn calls then. I've been trying to get hold of you for ages.'

'I had to answer a call of nature actually.'

Sheila knew Ron was lying but didn't push it.

'I've got a pick-up from Richmond Avenue - girl named Claire. Can you do it?'

Ron nodded to himself. He'd picked up Claire on previous occasions and taken her over the river. She was a lovely girl, originally from Yorkshire and down to earth. A good laugh and also a good tipper.

'That means I won't be able to pick-up Mrs Cooper later, though.' Mrs Cooper stayed over with her daughter every Thursday night and liked to get up early and return home before visiting her late husband's grave where, she'd told Ron, she hoped to join him in the not too distant future. She lived near Ron and it was convenient that she had become his last fare before he knocked off on a Friday morning.

'I'll get Mike to cover,' said Sheila and Ron smiled to himself. Sheila wasn't a bad sort. She knew he was saving to give Val a good holiday and young Claire's fare would earn him more than the old lady's. Every little helped as they said.

'Okay, no probs. I'll be there in,' he looked at his watch, 'fifteen minutes max.' They hung up and Sheila relayed the message to Claire.

16

It had been a perfect night and Claire wished she could play hooky and stay in bed with Jay all day. She snuck back under the duvet after calling for the taxi and Jay was still sleeping. She looked at his relaxed face and body only half covered by the quilt. Smiling in memory of how skilled he was with that body, she gently put the quilt over his exposed arm and torso and lightly kissed his cheek, not wanting to wake him.

He opened his eyes and grabbed her. After a long, lingering kiss they came up for air and Jay could see that Claire wasn't happy about leaving.

'I've got to work too, darling. Shall I make you a coffee before you go?'

God, he was such a catch. 'No thanks, babes, I'm fine. Go back to sleep for a bit and I'll see you tonight.'

They kissed one last time. Jay smiled and turned over. He was sleeping by the time Claire closed the door.

Although it was stupid o'clock in the morning she walked to the taxi with a spring in her step, looking forward to the weekend and making plans with Jay for the rest of their lives together.

'Hello, love,' said Ron when she jumped off the bottom two steps and fell into the back seat of the taxi.

'Bloody hell. Take it easy girl,' he said. 'Don't want you injured on my shift.'

She laughed as they pulled out onto the road. Despite the city being awake all night it was relatively quiet on the roads at this time in the morning. Claire looked at her watch wondering how long she should wait before calling her brothers to tell them how it went. She'd call her parents later on tonight when she knew her father would be home rather than speaking to him at work. The good news might cheer her mother up as she'd sounded a bit down just lately.

Ron looked in the mirror and thought his fare looked extremely pleased with herself.

'I can see somebody's had a good night, love. Care to…'

'Effing hell,' screamed Claire and Ron mounted the empty kerb, managing to dodge the car speeding in their direction, too far on the wrong side of the road.

'Bloody lunatic!' he shouted, honking his horn at the same time but it was over in a flash, the other vehicle long gone. His quick thinking had saved them from a head-on collision and Claire took a deep breath.

'Oh my God. I could have been killed on the same night my boyfriend proposed to me. That would have been…' she stopped to consider and smiled as Ron looked at her in the mirror. 'Shit, Ron. That's what that would've been. Great driving by the way.'

He acknowledged with a smile. 'Congratulations. When's the big day then? Oh, hang on.'

Ron's mobile started ringing and he leaned over to pick it up off the passenger seat, keeping one eye on the road. The phone fell to the floor.

'Shit.'

The roads were pretty quiet so Ron kept his right hand on the steering wheel as he fumbled on the floor with his left. If somebody was calling him at this time in the morning it must be pretty important so he had to answer it.

Claire saw the lights getting nearer and nearer. 'They're changing, Ron. Slow down. Slow down!'

Dave's filter light was on green and he'd manoeuvred half of his big truck through the right turn when he saw the taxi heading towards him. *Must have good brakes* was his first thought before he realized there was no way the car would stop at the lights so impact was inevitable. There was nowhere Dave could go and nothing he could do. His world turned to slow motion as he touched the cross that he always wore on his silver chain. The impact came and jolted the big truck but Dave managed to bring it to a halt and he said a silent prayer before jumping down from his cab and running to the gruesome scene.

*****

At 5.17 am Claire's twin brothers Tony and Jim awoke simultaneously in the flat they shared. Jim left his sleeping girlfriend Fiona in their bed, picked up his phone from the bedside cabinet and switched on its light. He slipped on a pair of tracksuit bottoms and t-shirt and quietly left the room. Something awful had happened to his sister. The light was already on in the kitchen and Tony was standing there, looking at his own phone when Jim entered.

'I've texted Tash. No reply,' said Tony. Neither thought it strange that they were both awake at the same time, worried about their sister, and didn't need to communicate their worries to each other.

'I'm going to phone her.'

Deep down they both knew their sister was gone but neither was ready to accept the inevitable.

Chapter 2

Claire surveyed the scene below her. Somehow she seemed to be up in the air, looking down at people in white coats in some sort of clinical environment.

'Where am I and what's going on?' She couldn't see anybody else and was surprised to hear Ron's voice.

'You don't know do you? I'm so sorry, love.'

'Where are you? Ron?'

Before he had a chance to answer Claire saw movement below and took another look. A package had been placed on a slab and one of the white coats unzipped the package and with the assistance of another, lifted a body out of the bag.

Claire was surprised but still didn't get it. 'Oh look, Ron. She looks a bit like me.'

Ron appeared next to her. At least, she thought it was Ron. He had an aura of Ron about him but didn't seem to be in his physical form somehow. Something very strange was going on and she needed to get it sorted. At this rate she'd be late for work and that would scupper her chances of an early Friday finish.

Then it clicked.

'I'm having a dream,' she said to herself. 'I've nodded off in the taxi and because of that little fright I'm dreaming that I'm dead.'

Then it really did click.

'Oh my God. Am I dead? Ron, where are you?'

Ron heard the panic in Claire's voice and realized she'd worked it out. Poor girl. She'd had her whole life ahead of her and he'd ruined it because of his demanding mobile phone.

'I'm so sorry, Claire. Really, really sorry.'

'Sorry,' shouted Claire. 'Bloody sorry! Sorry doesn't cut it buster. Wait 'til I get my hands on you I'll effing kill you!'

'Err, I hate to be the one to point this out, love,' said Ron, 'but I think you'll find you're a bit late for that.'

He heard Claire's scream and decided to leave her to it.

*****

He didn't know how it happened but the scene below him changed and he could see right into his house. Ron was gutted that he wouldn't be around to look after Val and to give her the holiday of her dreams for their 25th wedding anniversary. He was relieved that he had plenty of life insurance and hoped the policies would pay out even though his negligence had caused the accident. Ron looked down and could see her hugging herself and crying. He started wailing when it dawned on him that he'd never hold her again, play verbal table tennis or be around to look after her in their old age. Their daughter Libby walked into the bedroom and Val and Libby hugged. They tried to console each other but were too distraught to offer much comfort.

'It's all my fault,' said Val between sobs. 'If I'd been a better wife your father would still be alive.' Libby shook her head and carried on hugging her mother.

Ron wondered why Val was blaming herself as he watched his wife and daughter try to comfort each other. He sensed the presence behind him and without turning to look he knew it was Claire.

'Why does your wife think she's to blame?' asked Claire and he couldn't tell whether she'd calmed down since their last discussion or whether she was going easy on him because he was upset.

21

'Who knows? Maybe it's because we were going through a rough patch.' Ron felt tears and was surprised he could still cry when dead.

Claire wanted to put an arm around him but not yet used to her current state, wasn't quite sure how to do it. Ron felt the warmth of her hug without the physicality of it.

'Thanks, love,' he said, 'and I really am sorry about the, you know. If there's anything I can do to make it up to you, let me know.'

Claire laughed but it wasn't funny. 'I can't think of anything aside from rewinding time and not causing me to die,' she said.

'Point taken. Look,' said Ron, needing to change the subject and indicating the change in the scene below. 'You have visitors. Must be there to identify you before your post mortem. Coming for a look?'

Claire knew it would be very emotional but couldn't stop herself. They moved nearer and watched events unfold, just like me and Tash would do on a Monday night in, watching all the soaps, she thought.

*****

Jay refused to believe it.

Claire's twin brothers had picked him up and they had collected Tash on their way to the mortuary. Her parents were travelling down from Yorkshire and would meet them there. The twins sat quietly in the front, Tony driving and Jim looking out of the window. It was obvious they'd been crying but now they seemed to have turned inward and every time Jay spoke they merely grunted or gave one word answers, refusing or unwilling to get into a conversation. In contrast, Tash was sitting next to Jay bawling her eyes out. He knew that all this was one big misunderstanding and the body at the morgue would be that of a complete stranger, not his Claire.

They arrived and parked up. He took a deep breath and headed towards the main entrance in a hurry, not looking forward to the task but keen to establish it had all been one big mix-up. A story they would share with their kids in years to come. Jay wanted to go into the room alone so the others agreed to wait outside.

Tony and Jim stood next to each other and Tony put a hand on Jay's forearm before he entered.

'Claire's gone.'

Annoyed, Jay shrugged him off and walked towards the door.

Claire watched him enter the room and wanted to be there with him. Not sure how it had happened, she was now next to him, crying and explaining that she loved him and that it wasn't her fault she'd left. Jay stopped before he reached the trolley and shivered. He sensed her presence and knew instantly. The cold truth hit him like a bucket of iced water. As quickly as he'd sensed her presence it disappeared and his agony was too much for words. He let out a primal scream and collapsed to the floor.

Tony and Jim burst through the door closely followed by the mortuary staff. The twins gently lifted Jay and sat him down on a chair. Seeing the cover on her body still undisturbed they looked at each other and Jim nodded.

'Did you look, Jay?' said Tony, and Jay lifted his head and looked at her brothers. All colour had drained from his face but the twins were too anxious for information about their sister to worry about him.

'I didn't need to look.' He shook his head and folded his arms around his middle, pushing them into his stomach, trying unsuccessfully to stop the pain. 'She was in the room with me.'

Jim nodded his head and the twins looked at each other in silent understanding, but knowing that Claire had now left the room. They walked over to the trolley slowly, in perfect sync, and the mortuary attendant would later tell his colleagues how weird the whole experience had been from the comments of the dead girl's fiancé to her identical twin brothers who seemed able to mind read.

They'd been warned that the person on the trolley had suffered severe trauma and knew that Claire was under the cover but nothing could prepare them for the shock of seeing their sister's lifeless and broken body.

Claire was once again looking at the scene from above and had no idea how she'd travelled between the two places. She looked down at her mangled shell and was devastated by the sight. Devoid of life, her face was bruised and pale with a wide gash under her chin. The boys had slowly moved more of the sheet in morbid fascination, although they'd been advised not to, and Claire's legs sat at unnatural angles, obviously broken. She didn't want to watch any more but she felt drawn to the scene below her like a passing driver rubber-necking a road accident. She laughed bitterly to herself at the likeness. That was exactly what she was, a road accident, taken before her time and now only able to watch those she loved live life to the full instead of living it with them.

Her parents arrived shortly after. Claire barely recognized her mother who had aged considerably since she last saw her. They both wanted to see their daughter's body but the twins advised against it.

'You don't want this to be the final memory of her,' said Jim, trying his best not to break down in front

24

of everyone. The twins had vowed to be strong for the sake of their parents but were finding it difficult, especially as Tash hadn't stopped bawling and the noise was beginning to grate on everyone's nerves.

Graham, Claire's father, reached for his wife's hand but Marion ignored him and instead nodded to the mortuary attendant.

'This way please,' said the man in the white coat and walked through the door ahead of them. Marion took a deep breath as the cover was removed to expose her daughter's face. Her worst nightmares were confirmed. She looked at the broken body of her daughter. This was all wrong thought Marion wondering why nature had been reversed. Parents weren't meant to outlive their offspring.

'I've lost my daughter.' Marion muttered.

'Me too.' Graham tried to hold her but Marion was inconsolable and refused the contact.

'My only girl, my baby.' She shuddered then sobs wracked her whole body.

He tried again but his wife refused his attempts at physical contact. Graham stood with his arms by his side and his chin resting on his chest, staring at the face of his little princess. For once in his life he didn't know what to do. How could it be that his daughter had been taken away from them all on what should have been one of the happiest nights of her life? And why wouldn't Marion let them comfort each other? He stopped thinking and looked at what used to be his daughter. He allowed the numbness to take over, in an attempt to mask the great big hole that he felt spreading throughout his entire body.

Outside in the waiting area, Tash was still crying and Jay sat down, hugging himself. Tony entered the room and told his parents it was time to leave. They both followed him out like zombies in a cheap B Movie and Jay stood up as they came out. No words were exchanged between Jay and Claire's parents. They didn't know each other very well and Jay felt unable to offer Marion any physical comfort as she walked directly to the exit, still ignoring her husband and everyone else around her. Graham gripped the top of Jay's right arm and the two men looked at each other in painful understanding of what they'd lost. Graham pulled Jay into his arms and gave him a tight bear hug. Even under the circumstances the twins were amazed as their father was a typical old-fashioned Yorkshire man who very rarely showed any emotion. The men separated and tears slowly trickled down Jay's face. Having watched his wife shuffle out of the door and seeing the distraught youngsters in the room, something clicked inside Graham. He came out of his trance and went onto autopilot. He held Jay at arm's length and looked into his eyes.

'Be strong, son,' he said. 'I'll call you about the arrangements after the post mortem.' He turned to the twins. 'Do what you have to do today and then come home. Your mother needs you.' Graham put a hand on Tash's shoulder and she looked up at him and managed a weak smile. If Claire's father could be strong the least she could do was try. Graham followed his wife out of the door, knowing his family was broken and that he was the one who had to hold it together for all their sakes.

What he didn't know was that his safe, hidden secret was already out and his daughter's death was the catalyst that would cause his own life to implode.

*****

So this was it then. Life as she knew it was over. Her family had actually loved her after all and because she was dead, yes dead, they were all suffering and there was not a thing she could do about it. These were Claire's thoughts as her loved ones left the building.

Death means that I stay here for eternity as a spectator instead of one of the main cast.

She was shortly to discover her assumption about her future had been completely wrong.

Chapter 3

Claire could hear Ron's voice in the background but was having her favourite fantasy and didn't want it to end. It was their wedding day. They'd been lucky with the weather. It was warm, but not too warm, and the air was still. A few small clouds hung static in the deep blue sky. The elaborate white chairs padded and covered with red velvet, had been placed in rows of ten on the gravelled area beyond the country mansion's patio. Claire's family and friends were sitting chatting on the left side and Jay's on the right. A red carpet placed in between the rows of chairs led the way to the concrete steps at the top of which the ceremony would take place. Jay stood nervously talking to his best man awaiting the arrival of his beautiful bride. Claire and her bridesmaids, Tash and her best friend from school Cheryl, made their way from her room along the corridor towards the entrance. Although the listed building had been modernized it still contained the framework of its original features and the mix of old and new gave it a feeling of splendour and comfort. The front doors were already open and they didn't notice the wedding planner as he indicated that the guests should stand. All of the women turned to look at Claire and the men smiled at the 'Ooohs and Aaahs', knowing that there'd be tears spilt before the end of the ceremony.

Claire looked and felt wonderful. In her fantasy she'd managed to lose the five pounds that took her down to what she considered to be her ideal weight. She was in a tight fitting white satin dress that clung to her upper body, showing off her lovely figure. The sleeveless creation had a row of crystals sewn to the neckline, which shimmered in the sun. The dress billowed out from the waist and as Claire walked to meet her groom, the bottom half of her dress undulated like waves buffeted by a gentle breeze. Her bridesmaids followed behind holding her train. As she walked along the red carpet she locked eyes with Jay. It was as if an invisible thread held their look and they smiled at each other enjoying the moment. Claire took her eyes off Jay and handed her bouquet of freesias to Cheryl before walking up the steps. She was greeted by the Registrar and her groom, and taking in a breath, she took a moment to admire the stunning view from the elevated position, determined to enjoy every minute of the wonderful day. To the right was nothing but green countryside with gently sloping hills. On the other side was the magnificent sea view. The day could not have been more perfect.

'Claire. Claire. Come on! I need to speak to you.'

Ron's shouting shattered her fantasy and brought her back to the present with a depressing thump. When he saw her face he knew straight away that she'd been fantasizing. He had fantasized many times about his holiday with Val for their 25th wedding anniversary.

'Oh, Claire, it's going to be all right, you know.'

She couldn't hide her tears and she didn't want to.

'I thought I'd never know what it felt like to wear my wedding dress, to see what Jay looked like on our special day and to see how happy our friends and family were for us. But I was wrong. It was like I lived it, Ron, and it was so...' She shuddered and sucked in a few breaths, trying to find the right word to explain.

'It was just so real, as if I was actually there. But I'm not. I'm here and I'll never go on honeymoon with Jay. Never experience the pain and joy of childbirth. Never see the emotion on his face from holding our

29

sons and daughters. Never attend their school sports days, never...'

Her sobbing prevented her from continuing. Ron put his arms around her and stroked her hair, trying to console her. She felt real to him but both of them knew that this was some sort of illusion and that their physical bodies no longer existed. It didn't matter as long as they could pretend.

Thinking of the whole death experience it had not been what she'd expected to say the least. There hadn't been a tunnel, a white light or any of her dead relatives beckoning her or steering her in the right direction. The last was a disappointment. If she had to be dead the least that could be done was to reconnect her with her adored grandmother who had died more than two years before. She still felt as if she had a body and felt as if she could open and close her eyes yawn and stretch but yet, when she tried to look at herself, all she saw was a hovering light. It was all very weird and Claire wasn't yet used to her new status and situation.

The mood was broken by an interruption shortly after and they turned, looking in the direction where they'd heard a whoosh. A bright golden light appeared and both squinted as if the sun were blinding them. The light slowly began to take form and a female appeared in front of them. The light had made them feel wonderful and Claire and Ron instantly forgot their conversation as they surveyed the angel before them. Over six feet tall and dark as a moonless night, with long black tresses that were blowing over her face. Must have been a windy journey thought Claire, smiling. She was dressed in a gown and there were two large wings on her back but unlike any pictures that Claire had seen of angels, these wings were black and the feathers black, shiny and exquisite.

Her hair calmed and she smiled and Claire felt as if they were friends already.

'I'm Gabriella and as you might have guessed, I'm an angel. To simplify matters for you both, think of me as an Admin Angel and your guide and mentor. I have many tasks to complete so I need you to pay attention and to listen without interruption.' Gabriella lifted her hand and caught two notebooks, which had appeared out of nowhere. Claire and Ron were mesmerized, as if watching a magician.

'Get comfortable and I'll begin.'

Lovely as the angel was, Claire had many questions.

'Hang on a minute, I need to...'

'All will become clear, dear Claire.' She opened one of the books, scanning a page. Closing it she looked at Claire.

'Hmm... As I thought, impatience is one of your flaws. You will need to listen to the wisdom of others, Claire if you want to progress...'

'But I...'

'Just listen for a minute, love,' said Ron and Claire didn't say a word but leaned her head to one side, raised her eyebrows and pursed her lips while looking at Gabriella.

'You are not a child, Claire, though we are all children of the Chairman,' said Gabriella, and Claire's good feelings towards her were beginning to waiver.

'Neither are you a teenager and you should not expect all your own way.' She lifted her hand containing the book into the air and waved it.

Learning that her anger wouldn't get her anywhere with the angel, Claire tried to calm down.

'Shall we carry on or shall I come back at a later date?'

'Please carry on,' said Ron, and Claire nodded, not trusting herself to comment.

'For every one of you that arrives, a decision has to be made whether to recommend you to upstairs

31

or to downstairs, for eternity. We take into consideration a number of factors such as your behaviour before arrival and the circumstances of your journey to us.'

It seemed pretty clear to Claire and Ron so far, though neither had imagined that this was how it would be.

'As you can imagine, we are very busy and the more souls we have to deal with at any given time the longer it takes to come to a decision. I'm afraid I have something very distressing to show you.'

Claire doubted that anything could be more distressing than having her life cut short in the way that she had but had no choice other than to listen to the angel.

Gabriella explained that the events they were about to watch had started during the night of their death. She hung her head in obvious grief and her emotion was almost palpable. She made a sweeping motion with her arm and they watched a scene unfold below them.

A large ship was moored in the sea, the passengers enjoying themselves on the deck, sunbathing, swimming and relaxing after having visited an island.

'A cruise,' said Claire and the others ignored her.

The calm sea started agitating and the passengers looked around, feeling the ship's movements. This was unusual in itself on such a big liner. None of them knew the cause, thankfully, until the wave hit. Thousands of tons of water shattered the massive cruise liner as if it were plywood. The screams were drowned out by the noise of the water.

'Three thousand, seven hundred and fifty-four,' said Gabriella.

Claire covered her open mouth with a hand and Ron remained silent as they looked on in awe and distress as the wave hit land and caused immeasurable devastation.

'Can you stop it now please?' she said as they watched first hundreds, then thousands of people lose their lives in the violence and carnage of the tsunami.

Further scenes were displayed once the wave had dissipated. Broken homes and people. Toddlers crying unable to understand what had happened and with nobody available to comfort them.

'Enough, please,' said Claire.

'I thought they could predict them these days and save lives,' said Ron and Gabriella told him that an unusual earthquake had happened on the seabed causing the tsunami and that it wasn't always possible to predict nature.

'How many?'

'Including those at sea, fourteen thousand and thirty-one. We're expecting many more to arrive in the aftermath because of disease,' said Gabriella, 'and it would have been worse had not the Committee caused the diversion that stopped even more people arriving on the island.' Gabriella explained that the Committee had arranged a large storm that had stopped flights from arriving on the island.

'If they can arrange storms then why can't they stop earthquakes and tsunamis?' It was a logical question and Gabriella explained that some weather events could be arranged or managed but not geological occurrences.

'Poor people,' said Claire. Both she and Ron were upset at what they'd witnessed and Gabriella wanted to give them time to gather their thoughts.

'I'll come back later and we'll talk some more,' she said before disappearing in a whoosh as suddenly as she'd arrived but this time without the bright light.

'It's awful, Ron. All those people and such a violent death.' Claire was still upset about her own death but this had given her something else to dwell on. Ron agreed. Their own deaths had been violent but thankfully without much pain.

'And what did she mean by the Committee and the Chairman?' Claire often asked questions that Ron couldn't answer so, consumed by his own thoughts and grief, he quietly ignored her.

Neither knew how much time had passed before they heard another of the whooshes which preceded Gabriella's arrival. She continued speaking as if she hadn't left.

'In addition to this disaster...'

'Who are the Committee?'

'Let me finish, Claire' said Gabriella. 'The next part may be even more difficult to bear.'

She couldn't imagine why but waited nervously.

'While we were all very busy following the Committee's instructions and trying to limit the death toll of the earthquake and tsunami, I'm sure you can appreciate that we weren't able to monitor everything on Earth?'

Sounded reasonable and they nodded.

'There's no easy way to tell you this but Ron was actually meant to bring Mrs Cooper with him.' She hesitated. 'And you, Claire, were meant to carry on with your life on Earth.'

Claire looked at them both, the bloody incompetent taxi driver and the beautiful black angel who had calmly informed her that she should still be alive. She felt a rage that she hadn't known before, even worse than when the *Next* sale had started and a woman had taken the only size 12 black sparkly top out of her hands. A volcano was erupting inside her and Claire muttered a number of chosen expletives. Gabriella informed her that under no circumstances was this sort of behaviour permitted. Ignoring the angel, she lashed out, screaming then shouting and thrashing at them both and anything else that she could see around her. She felt a sharp painful prod and then nothing.

*****

Claire opened her eyes. She felt rough and didn't know how much time had passed since she'd lost her temper. She was on her own and contemplated the information she'd been given. She understood that if further attention had been given to her predicament there would have been additional deaths as a result of the earthquake and tsunami. She had therefore been sacrificed so that many other people could live. Claire was glad that others hadn't died but still felt cheated. She loved and missed her family and friends but that was nothing compared to what she felt at losing Jay. Every part of her soul ached for him and Claire thought she'd be consumed with grief forever. She still felt like she'd been cheated of a future and however much she tried, couldn't get rid of the anger that was constantly bubbling under the surface. If this was what eternity was all about then the angels, Committee and Chairman, whoever they were, could shove it where the sun didn't shine!

As Claire wondered what was happening at home it was as if a massive screen opened below her and she watched with interest.

*****

Tash was sitting on Claire's bed, crying.

'I'm so sorry... So sorry!' she repeated over and over and didn't bother to wipe away her tears. After a little while she stood up and gave a mighty sigh. She ran a hand down her black dress, ensuring that it was crease free, then walked to the dressing table to check her eyes in the mirror. They were bloodshot but the waterproof mascara had done its job and hadn't run at all. Tash returned to her own room, put on her black jacket and pinned the black fascinator to her hair. She heard a honk outside and after checking it was the taxi made her way downstairs.

Jim and Tony were outside the church and Jim's girlfriend was inside, seated in the row behind their parents. Tony opened the door when the taxi stopped. He looked at Tash and wondered if she had meant to attend a society wedding then remembered it was his sister's funeral and she hadn't had time to change.

'It's Claire's funeral,' was all he managed to say and Tash frowned.

'Yes, Tony. That's why I'm here.'

'Go into the church and say hello to my parents. Then sit in the pew behind them with Fiona.' Surprised at Tony's curtness, she asked if Jay had arrived.

'He's with them.' Tony turned and re-joined his brother who was leaning against a wall, smoking a cigarette. He offered one to his twin, who accepted. Tash was surprised, as both were super fit and health freaks. She hadn't realized that either of them smoked, Jim certainly didn't in work. Tony had seemed odd and distant too but that was understandable she supposed, under the circumstances.

She entered the church and approached Jay and Claire's parents. As soon as they turned to face her Tash saw the guilt on Jay's face and, though Claire's parents were shrouded in pain, she noticed their expressions change when they saw her. Tash knew that Jay had told them. *Shit*, she thought as she went to embrace Claire's mother. Marion took a step back and Tash almost overbalanced. Embarrassed at the reaction she righted herself and muttered how sorry she was to both of them.

Turning to Jay she said in barely a whisper, 'Can we talk later?'

Before Jay had a chance to answer, Marion spoke. 'You should both be ashamed of yourselves. She adored you, Jay and Tash. Claire would have trusted the both of you with her life.'

Tash ran out of the church sobbing. Other guests turned and stared, wondering about the commotion and assuming that the loss of her best friend was all too much for the poor girl. Jay looked at Graham and Marion.

'I shouldn't have told you. I'm so sorry. You have to believe me that it was a mistake early on in our relationship and I'll always love Claire. I'm so, so, sorry.' Jay put his head in his hands and sobs wracked his body. It was the second time that he'd cried since she'd died, the first when they visited her body. He wished he hadn't told Marion about his mistake. He'd been so drunk and couldn't even remember how he told her. Alcohol was the only thing that numbed the pain and he knew he'd relied on it too much since Claire's death. He still couldn't believe that he'd never see her again and he promised himself that he would stay sober on the day of her funeral, so there was nothing to numb the pain today.

Graham put a supporting hand on his shoulder and Jay tried to get a grip. Graham seemed a lot more understanding than Marion, which was funny in a non-humorous way as Claire had been a Daddy's girl and idolized by her father. Graham had given him a proper bollocking but seemed to know that it had been a one-off mistake - a stupid reaction following a horrendous argument - and was able to forgive him. He didn't think that Marion would ever forgive him. He'd got on well with the twins up to now but assumed that Marion had told them, as they were both cold and distant. Saying that, Jay knew that the twins had loved and always tried

37

to protect their little sister and they all had a weird sixth sense thing going on between them. They'd arranged for her to move to her flat which was only a 5-minute walk from their own. They seemed to have turned inward since she'd left, communicating almost telepathically with each other, and only talking to others as and when it was absolutely necessary. Jim was lucky that his girlfriend was so understanding. At least he had her support. Jay turned and watched Tash re-enter the church. He couldn't forgive himself for cheating on Claire and, after going to the flat to clear out her belongings with Graham the following week, he never wanted to see Tash again.

The coffin bearers, Graham, Jay, the twins and Claire's twin cousins placed the casket at the front of the church and the service began. It took approximately one hour for family and friends to say goodbye to the 24-year-old who had had so much going for her and been taken so cruelly from this world to the next – according to the minister. *I Will Always Love You* rang out from the CD player as Claire's casket disappeared behind curtains. It now seemed real and final to Jay and the family and Marion was inconsolable. The men tried their best to retain some composure while saying goodbye to some of the family who had to return to their homes in Yorkshire ready for work the following day, and were unable to attend the wake. The remainder of the solemn guests returned to their transport and headed for the hotel where her father was determined that they would celebrate her life, as well as grieving her death.

*****

Gobsmacked was the first word that sprang to mind as the image below blurred and the scene slowly faded away. Just when she thought that nothing could possibly make her feel any worse she'd been wrong yet again and the volcano inside her started to well up once more. So her fiancée had cheated on her with her best friend. Claire almost felt like a cliché. She could forgive her parents for holding her funeral in a church – even though she was a non-believer she understood that religion was a crutch for her mother and she might have found some comfort in it. Following her upset the realization of what Jay and Tash had done to her hit home. Claire felt as cold and hard as steel as she wondered if there was anything she could do in her current situation, to show them how much they'd hurt her.

*****

As she was pondering revenge Ron appeared, quickly followed by Gabriella, after the now customary whoosh.

Gabriella noted Claire's changed demeanour but chose to ignore it for the time being. 'I need you to listen, without interruption, and you can ask any questions once I've finished. Understand?' She didn't wait for them to answer. 'I explained that we have to process every soul that comes here and due to the disaster we're all very busy.' Noting they were paying attention, she continued.

'Death so far is probably not what you expected?'

They nodded, noting that Gabriella was very business-like.

'You are currently in *Cherussola*. This is where your future is determined and the Committee decide whether you go upstairs or downstairs.'

'Cherussola,' said Claire, 'what does that mean?'

Gabriella ignored the question so she tried again. 'Are we in a sort of Halfway House?'

'Yes, between heaven and hell, I think,' Ron whispered and Claire raised her eyebrows.

39

'Ron, in your fifty-three years on Earth you have made a few mistakes...'

'You bet he has,' said Claire, recalling their demise.

'It was predetermined,' said Ron, 'and out of my control if you remember what Gabriella told us.'

'Silence!' Her change of tone shocked them both and they straightened and looked at the angel, concerned at the consequences of non-compliance.

'As I was saying,' she returned to sweetness and light. 'Ron, all in all you have been kind, considerate and giving during your last lifetime. You have learnt much from your previous lives and still have a little to learn but you have a good soul and will eventually go upstairs and experience a wonderful eternity.'

Ron wanted to ask a question but was fearful of irritating Gabriella. He raised a hand as if in a classroom.

'Go ahead.'

'What do you mean, 'last lifetime'?'

'When the Chairman and Committee are undecided about which eternity a soul should have, they send individuals back to Earth to live additional lives. Eventually the true nature of the soul will show and for those who've lived to your age it can be a relatively easy decision. You'll discover more of your previous lives when I send you upstairs.'

Ron's mind was buzzing with loads of unanswered questions and he raised his hand again.

'My time with you is limited. Just relax for now, Ron.' Gabriella bestowed an angelic smile and his questions disappeared. He felt at peace and was relieved that this wasn't his final resting place. He relaxed and listened.

'Claire, your situation is more complex.'

Claire started to worry. She thought about the time she'd broken a window and had convinced her

40

parents that it was her brothers who'd done it. They'd been grounded for a week and lost their pocket money. Okay, so they'd locked her under the stairs the first time they babysat for her when her parents were out and told her that the spiders would kill her. Come to think of it they'd also told her that she'd been adopted because her real father was a murderer and she'd cried herself to sleep that night. But Claire reflected it wasn't her brothers who were on trial here for their future. It was her.

She recalled other events in her life where she had not covered herself in glory. Louisa, the fat kid in her class in secondary school was a prime example. The bullies had teased and taunted Louisa and Claire had not done anything to put a stop to it. On one occasion she'd even laughed with them. Louisa left the school and Claire heard that she'd suffered from anorexia in her later teenage years. Then there was the boy who stuttered and some of the same gang used to take the mickey out of him.

She'd also pulled a cat's tail when she was young and remembered being at a bus stop with Tash, laughing at a woman who was unaware that she had a snot hanging from her nostril.

'Enough!' said Gabriella and Claire looked up, wondering if she could read her thoughts.

'Firstly, you were too young and too fickle in this life for your final location to be determined. Secondly, as I've already said, you were brought here purely by accident and it was not yet your time.'

Difficult as it was, Claire resisted the urge to interrupt and listened intently.

'There are other factors in your situation, Claire, that make the Committee's decision a difficult one. They may have to refer you to the Chairman but have decided to put your case on hold for the time being. In the meantime, the many other Admin Angels and I will deal with the backlog caused by the recent disaster.'

Almost fit to burst with curiosity, Claire was finding it increasingly difficult to remain quiet. She assumed that Gabriella was aware of that as she felt as if she could almost read her soul.

'Now you may ask questions.'

'But that can't be it. There must be more. What's going to happen? What do I do?'

'You're right, Claire, that's not it. For cases like yours we have a procedure.'

Most of the time since her death had not been good and Claire silently wished for a change of luck.

'You could actually consider yourself quite lucky as you will have opportunities not given to many who pass through here. While you remain until a final decision is made you will be able to make return visits to Earth,' Gabriella paused and pointed at Claire.

'How you decide to make the best of your time during those visits is up to you, but remember what I've already told you. Ron, you will keep Claire company for the time being. And this...' she moved her arm in a sweeping motion, indicating their current home. 'With a little practice and imagination you can make it as comfortable or uncomfortable as you wish.'

Both attempted to ask further questions but Gabriella silenced them with a look then leaned back and studied them intently. 'You may find things a little difficult on your first visits but I'll leave that up to you to discover. Good luck and,' she smiled angelically, 'remember that somebody may be watching you.'

They heard the whoosh and Gabriella disappeared. Neither spoke for a while as they contemplated the information given to them. Ron eventually broke the silence.

'So, basically I'm babysitting you until they decide whether you're going to heaven or hell.' He didn't sound too happy to Claire.

'Actually, Ron, I think it's the least you can do under the circumstances. And anyway, you know where you're going to end up – so how do you think I feel?'

She had a point and he moved toward her wanting to give her some comfort. It was awkward at first, then he hugged her and she was grateful to him, it made her feel a bit better. She still held him partly responsible for her death but her anger toward him had diminished since they'd discovered that her arrival there had been a mistake. Claire started to feel excited too. She'd be able to visit Earth, catch up with those she loved and, hopefully, repay a few outstanding debts.

*****

Jay was waiting down the road from the flat. He didn't want to go in until Graham arrived, having no desire to be on his own with Tash. As soon as he saw Claire's father he rushed to meet him and the two men prepared themselves for the grizzly task of collecting and clearing all of Claire's belongings. Tash answered the door and appeared not to want to be near Jay. She gave them a set of keys and excused herself, saying that she was meeting a friend. Both men hovered in the kitchen, wanting the task to be over, but neither really wanting to start. It was the third day since Claire's death that Jay had been completely sober. Every morning he woke forgetting that she was no longer with him and each day was like Groundhog Day, with his heart breaking anew all over again. The only thing that numbed the pain was alcohol and Jay had come to rely on its anaesthetic qualities. Without it he had to face the stark reality of a life without the woman he loved and that was the situation he was in when he opened the door to her room, with her father standing behind him. The smell was the first thing that hit him. The

43

faint sweet odour of her perfume still lingered and Jay felt the groan rising up within him. Claire's dressing table was directly opposite the door and the first thing that her fiancé saw was the framed photograph of them both enjoying themselves at the Valentine's Day party earlier that year. Jay had exactly the same photograph framed in his apartment and the memories of the night came flooding back to him. The pain was too much and he doubled over, hugging himself and trying to stop the animal-like noises that he seemed unable to control.

'Come on, son,' said Graham, taking his arm and leading him out of the room. 'It's too soon. We'll do it another day.'

They returned to the kitchen and Graham made coffee while Jay tried to get a grip on himself. Graham told Jay that they could meet the following week to sort the room but knew even as he was saying it, that it would be too much for Jay. He decided he would ask his sons or Tash for help. They eventually said goodbye and went their separate ways, Graham worried about Jay but unable to do anything to improve his situation.

*****

A few weeks later Claire and Ron were surprised to find themselves in Claire's flat. Tash was out and Claire had a good look around. Her bedroom had been stripped of her belongings and looked sad and bare. She'd watched Jay and her father try to collect her stuff and her heart would have broken had she been alive. It had been easier when Tash had volunteered to do it, as Claire still felt annoyed at her friend's betrayal. Now she felt indifferent as if she were watching a movie of what someone else's life had been, not her own.

'She's coming,' said Ron, and Claire turned when she heard the key in the door.

Tash was on her mobile when she entered the flat. She kicked the door closed behind her and put her shopping bags on the floor. Claire wondered why she was home early from work but soon stopped that thought when Tash looked directly to where Claire was standing. She panicked, wondering how her former best friend could see her when Gabriella had assured them both that they would be invisible except to a few *special people*.

Tash carried on the conversation. 'I'm really sorry but I have to go. Can you come round at 6 pm?' She quickly finished the call and put her keys and mobile in her pocket and opened the flat's front door. With the door open so that she could exit quickly if she needed to, Tash walked stealthily to the kitchen and grabbed the long black-handled knife from the drawer.

'Hello. Anybody there?' she called.

'She means business,' said Claire to Ron and they watched as she checked every room, moving more confidently now that she held the sharp knife.

'She must sense something,' said Ron and Claire agreed.

'Weird,' muttered Tash when she'd checked all the rooms. She shook herself and gave a little laugh as she looked at the knife in her hand, feeling a bit silly for thinking someone was there. She closed the front door and after unpacking the shopping she spent the next few hours cleaning the flat from top to bottom. Claire wondered what was going on. Tash thought of housework as an extreme sport and would do anything to avoid it.

There was a knock on the door and it soon became clear to the spirits that Tash was interviewing potential new flatmates. This would be interesting.

'Hi, Elaine?' asked Tash and the short bespectacled woman dressed in brown trousers, cream

45

blouse, tartan coat, and wearing flat shoes (that Tash wouldn't be seen dead in) nodded her head. They shook hands and she invited her into the flat.

'Can I take your coat?'

'Ooh, it's a bit chilly,' said Elaine as she buttoned up her coat, looked around the hallway and shivered. 'Purple's a lovely colour but you could do with a lighter colour here. Makes small spaces look bigger you know.'

'I'll bear that in mind,' said Tash, trying not to let her first impressions cloud her judgement.

Claire was watching in amusement as the prim and proper Elaine criticized every room they entered. It was the most fun she'd had since she'd died. That was until they entered her old room. Elaine ran her forefinger over the dressing table then rubbed it with her thumb. She smiled condescendingly.

'Not sure about the green walls and it's clean on the surface but if I moved in it would need a proper deep clean first.'

'Well, thanks for coming,' said Tash looking at her watch. 'I'm sorry it doesn't suit but never mind. Nothing ventured, eh?'

'But I didn't say *it doesn't suit*,' said Elaine. 'I'm still thinking about it.'

'Trust me. You don't need to think any further,' said Tash as she chivvied Elaine out of the flat.

'Cheerio.' And she closed the door on the bemused woman. 'Give me strength,' she muttered, looking up at the ceiling, then turning her head toward the kitchen and walking quietly to the door to look inside. She didn't know what she expected to see but felt as if someone was there. Seeing nobody, she shook herself then hurried to the lounge and switched on the iPod. She couldn't get rid of the feeling that she was being watched. It was probably because Claire was on her mind due to the search for a new flatmate, thought

46

Tash, trying to think logically. She vowed to get a grip and waited for the next potential flatmate to arrive.

Claire had mixed feelings. The next one, Fran, seemed a lovely girl and was getting on well with Tash. She was normal, friendly with a sense of humour and looked as if she would be good fun. Claire knew that Tash would offer Fran the room and she was surprised to feel the first stirrings of jealousy. She was also surprised to discover that although she hadn't forgiven her, she missed Tash and the times they'd shared - both good and bad. Sensing Claire's mood change, Ron decided it was time for a distraction.

'Come on. We're leaving,' he said and before Claire had time to think about it, they were gone. She hadn't been ready to leave but it appeared she didn't have a choice.

'How did you do that?'

'Gabriella gave me a few tips that she didn't share with you. She knows how wilful you can be at times so it's a bit of a safety net.'

Having only visited Tash, she'd been putting off visits to Jay and her family for a while, knowing how painful they would be. But now she felt ready to make a start.

'I want to see Jay. Are you coming with me, Ron?'

'Of course,' he answered.

*****

Ken's skin was crawling and he was still terrified as he opened his eyes to view his new surroundings. It was very dark and some images rushed past him while others appeared in front of him. The hands that had brought him to his present destination started to grow bodies and they were all grotesque. He heard someone or something clear its throat and Ken

47

felt a thick liquid hit him, where one of his ankles used to be. He bent down to wipe it away and a deep commanding voice shouted.

'Leave it.'

Ken had no intention of arguing and the clearing throat noise became unbearable. He couldn't stand it and started to move.

'Stand still,' commanded the voice in barely more than a whisper and Ken stood while the thick viscous liquid multiplied around him and the last thing he remembered was being in a sea of the disgusting stuff, trying to keep his head above it. *How can I drown if I'm already dead?* was his final thought.

Some time later, Ken wished that he had drowned in the mass of phlegm. Standing alone in a dark room, the voices terrified him. Yet again he couldn't see who was speaking and wondered what would happen next.

It was quiet and he decided to move. He shouted in pain as he was prodded and hit by a bolt of electricity. He wondered if this was how animals felt and remained ramrod still for what seemed like an interminable period.

Eventually, someone or thing decided to speak. 'Return to Earth and attack your ex- lover,' commanded the same voice that had spoken earlier.

Ken uttered the first thought that popped into his head. 'Why?' He received a further shock for his curiosity and screamed.

'Okay, okay. Which one? Val?'

No response.

'All right. I'll do it.' Anything to get out of this place, thought Ken, and they weren't to know if he didn't follow through.

'He's failed,' said the voice and Ken was confused. He'd told them he'd do anything, why wouldn't they let him go? It took him a while to work

48

out that they could read his thoughts, then he knew he had no chance.

'He's no good to us here and he's boring me. Make him do something to entertain me.' A different voice this time, filled with evil and finality, and Ken shuddered when he heard it. There was no hope and he was very frightened.

It took him a while to realize that he had been returned to Earth. So many things were wrong that he didn't know where to start. His view of the scenery around him was from floor level and he couldn't see properly. His body wasn't right either and he felt a growing sense of panic. He didn't have much time to think as he saw two big feet approach and his automatic reaction was to take flight.

Ken landed on a piece of bread. He laid some of his own faeces onto the buttered bread, added liquid and proceeded to mash the contents together. Satisfied that his food was ready, he started eating and was ashamed to admit that he quite enjoyed it. He sensed a movement out of the corner of his eye and quickly flew from the plate and missed being swatted by a nano-second.

'Damn,' said the owner of the swatter. Ken flew onto the window and for reasons beyond his comprehension flew up and down the glass for a good few minutes. He disappeared once more when he saw the swatter approach and suddenly felt cold. He looked at his new surroundings, which appeared to be some sort of outhouse. Although choked that he had come back as a fly, he had no desire to return to the terrifying place he'd been taken since death and his survival instincts kicked in. He felt shattered and knew that if he didn't rest shortly he would drop, so he made his way to a corner of the room. Ken thought he'd be safely hidden and approached the area in haste. By the time his mind registered that he was about to land on a silvery web, he was going too fast to change direction. Plop. He landed and was instantly stuck. Despite his best efforts he couldn't move at all and he didn't know how long has passed when he felt a slight tremor in the web. The tremor changed to a vibration and he looked at the massive arachnid in terror. The spider either couldn't hear or ignored his pleading and quickly and efficiently wrapped Ken up in her strong silk. She gave her beautiful handiwork a satisfied look and disappeared to the other side of the web, where Ken noticed another wrapped parcel. He watched in horror as the spider unwrapped her other victim and hungrily devoured it. Had he had room to move he would have started shaking, but he was swathed too tightly, like an Egyptian Mummy. She came for him much later when he was barely conscious, and took him to levels of indescribable and unimaginable pain.

*****

Jay was sleeping on the sofa, music blaring from the speakers and an empty bottle by his side. Claire was confused. She thought it was a Wednesday but it must have been the weekend and Jay must really be suffering to be so out of it. She'd been dead for almost 4 months now and he shouldn't be in this state.

'Jay? Jay?' She couldn't help herself but he didn't stir.

He was walking down a country lane and the sun was shining. He looked to the woman standing next to him and smiled. It was Claire. She was back and she hadn't died. Jay woke up and the stark reality hit him. His head was pounding. He needed the bathroom and Claire was still dead. He relieved himself and went to the kitchen to get a glass of water. Two painkillers later he still didn't feel human. If only the tablets could take away the pain that had become a constant companion since he'd viewed her broken body. He looked at the bottle and Claire watched him, knowing exactly what he was thinking. She looked at Ron and he could see her distress. They reached an understanding without saying anything to each other. Concentrating hard their efforts paid off.

Jay opened the bottle. Before he could empty the tablets into his hand the bottle flew from him and landed on the floor. He went to pick it up and it moved. His confused brain told him that the bottle shouldn't be moving unaided but he was still drunk and focused on trying to retrieve the tablets. He attempted to pick up the bottle a further three times before giving up.

'What the fuck,' he said before returning to the living room and lying down to sleep. He hoped he'd have another lovely dream about Claire. Even in his drunken stupor it had felt so real.

Jay's hope was in vain though she did come to him again in his sleep. He was sitting on a bench in the park not far from his home. Claire walked towards him and he smiled. She reached him and sat down next to him. He could see she wasn't happy but didn't know why. She slapped his face.

'You two-timing bastard.'

That was all she said before she stood up and walked away. Jay woke sobbing his heart out. That had been an awful nightmare and he went to the bathroom to splash some water on his face hoping it would bring him round. He took a step back in shock when he saw the red mark on his face. He studied it intently, sobering up instantly. The handprint was clear and there was no way it could be anything else. Then his hung-over brain recalled the tablet bottle moving of its own volition and realization dawned. He knew for a fact that Claire had been there to stop him killing himself even though she knew he'd slept with Tash. He'd let her down. He also knew that she wouldn't want him to waste his life. From now on he'd stop wallowing in self-pity and make the most of his life. That was the least he could do for her. He made himself a strong black coffee and took a pen and notepad out of the drawer. For the first time in ages he noticed the build-up of dust on all the surfaces, the dishes stacked in the sink and the unpleasant smell in his flat. *Clean up* was the first thing he wrote on the list and he walked to the kitchen and filled the sink with hot water. Dishes first followed by everything else. Claire wouldn't want him living like this.

'So, your ex-fiancé is suicidal and you think that visiting him in a dream, calling him a two-timing bastard and slapping him is the way ahead?' said Ron when they were back at Cherussola.

Claire was exhausted and keen to end the conversation.

'I didn't know that he'd see me. I thought about it to make myself feel better and it just sort of happened.' She yawned. She had no idea how she'd made herself appear in Jay's dream but now she knew she could do it she was determined that it wouldn't be a one-off.

'And anyway, it's made him pull himself together and I'm not so worried about him now.' Claire couldn't say anything else. She struggled to remain with Ron but lost the fight. She drifted, trying to claw her way back to no avail. Then oblivion took her.

Ron watched as Claire slowly disappeared. He was relieved that Jay was feeling better but knew there'd be a time when he'd have to rein in Claire's impulsiveness. He wasn't looking forward to that day. Now that she'd gone he could relax without having to concern himself with what Claire would get up to while interfering in the lives of her family and friends.

Chapter 4

Four months had passed since Claire's funeral and Graham arrived home from work for the weekend. Marion was still cold and distant and Graham had reached a decision. He was going to come clean about his Monday to Friday life and the result of working away for so many years. He knew she'd be shocked but since Claire's death, he'd wondered about the purpose of life and was fed-up with the deceit. It was the least Marion deserved.

She heard the key in the door and sighed, the corners of her mouth turning downwards. Marion should have been glad to see her husband but nothing had made her happy since Claire's death and, if she was totally honest with herself, she hadn't been happy in their marriage for years. The twins had settled back into their work routine now and although they were still devastated about their sister, at least they'd stopped smoking and were being sensible again. This was in part due to Fiona and Marion was grateful to her.

'Marion, are you in?' His voice shook her out of her reverie and Marion turned to face the door. She stood up straight and folded her arms. He was in for a shock of his own this weekend, and he would get exactly what he deserved. Sweet FA!

Graham looked at his wife and realized this wasn't going to be easy.

Marion was in combative mode and didn't plan on taking any prisoners. He was going to pay, and pay dearly, for ruining the best years of her life.

'We need to talk.' They said it in unison and Graham noted that Marion's smile didn't reach her eyes. He was surprised that she hadn't asked how his week had been. She usually did though without even pretending to listen to the answer.

'I'll go first,' said Marion indicating that Graham should take a seat as if he were a guest and not in his own home.

'I have something to say,' replied Graham, hands on hips and standing his ground. He knew it was childish but didn't wish to be usurped by his wife.

Marion carried on as if he'd said nothing. 'I've been to see a solicitor.' That shut him up, she thought. 'And I want a divorce.'

Shocked into silence, Graham looked at his wife open mouthed and wide eyed.

'But...'

'I know all about Carol and your other life and I want you to leave my house. Do you hear me? MY HOUSE!'

Graham's head was spinning. Two minutes ago he would have laughed had anyone said that Marion would leave him. He'd wanted to leave for years but somehow just hadn't got around to it. And how did she know about Carol and what about Mel? Did she know about her as well? It was as if she'd read his mind and Marion's voice ended any further speculation.

'I also know that you still have a daughter and I don't. I hope your fancy piece has got an income as I'm taking what's rightly mine. Because of what you've done to me, Graham, I intend to fight you for every single item we own and the more miserable and unhappy that makes you, the happier I'll be.'

Marion smiled that smile again and took in a lungful of air.

'Now get out of my house. My solicitor will be in touch. I never want to speak to you again.'

Graham's mind was reeling. 'Let me explain, Marion...'

Marion balled her hand into a fist and banged it onto the table making him wince.

'Get out. Now!'

Graham had never seen his wife so livid, yet in control. It scared him, but not enough to make him move. Not until objects started flying through the air toward him.

He just managed to dodge the Lladro lady which hit the glass-topped side table with incredible force, shattering both the glass and the ornament itself.

Christ, what was she doing? thought Graham. He knew she loved that ornament.

Next came the small carriage clock that the firm had presented to him after 25 years with them. That was a direct hit to his left elbow and Graham yelled in protest. He made it through the door as a third object hit causing damage to the door he was sure, but he didn't stop to check.

Marion slapped her hands together once she'd heard the front door slam and looked around the room. Her home usually looked like a show house but now the lounge looked like the aftermath of a terrorist attack. Instead of feeling concerned Marion smiled to herself. That had felt good and for the first time since Claire's death she hadn't thought about her daughter for a few minutes. The intense pain returned with thoughts of Claire. Marion sat on her settee, put her head in her hands, and sobbed.

*****

Graham put his weekend bag back into the car and drove as if being chased by the devil. He stopped at the first service station on the motorway and ordered a coffee to drink in the car. Trying to collect his thoughts, what had happened with Marion seemed like a dream. Now that his marriage was actually over Graham wasn't sure how he felt. He knew he needed somewhere to stay and called Carol.

Carol saw his name display on the mobile and ran up the stairs to take the call.

'So you want to come home for the weekend? It's a bit short notice.' She tried to keep the surprise out of her voice. The only times he'd stayed the weekend during the past fifteen years had been for Mel's birthdays or other special occasions when she'd made a fuss, and these occasions had been planned well in advance. Something was up.

'I'll explain when I get there, but we need to talk. Can Mel stay with a friend tonight?'

Carol explained that Mel was staying with a friend from boarding school that weekend so wouldn't be home. It wasn't Mel that Carol would have to get rid of and she hesitated, trying to think of a solution.

'Carol? You there, Carol?'

'Yes of course. Actually, Graham. It's not very convenient this weekend, I have plans.'

'What do you mean you have plans? I need to stay and I need to talk to you, Carol.'

'I'm going away for the weekend,' said Carol, clutching at straws. 'To Butlins with some friends, sorry love.'

Graham was a little put out but not too bothered. He could do with some time on his own to get his head around his current situation.

'Not a problem. I'll stay at the house anyway until you get back.'

'No. No you can't. One of the reasons I'm going away is because I'm getting new windows put in downstairs. It's Roger's firm and they're working Saturday and Sunday so it will be finished by the time I get back.'

'Okay,' said Graham, smelling a rat. 'I'll see you Monday evening.'

They hung up and Carol was relieved that he'd accepted her story.

'Everything all right, love?' he shouted from the living room and she answered that it was fine and that

56

she'd be down in a minute. She went to the bathroom and checked her face. Her colour was normal and she smiled and made her way downstairs. That had been a close one and she wondered why she lied to him about Roger when he had his own double-life. The only one it wasn't really fair on was Roger. It wasn't the first time that Carol wondered why she didn't make a clean break from Graham and have an honest and serious relationship with kind, dependable Roger.

Two hours later Graham arrived unexpectedly and discovered that the rat he had smelled was named Roger. Roger left them to it and Carol was furious that Graham had spoiled her weekend life. He was mad that she'd been deceiving him.

'Let me get this right,' she said, hands on hips and scowling. 'You can have a whole other life and family, but I have to sit here on my own when you're not about, like a good little woman?'

'It's the deceit, Carol. I have never deceived you. And I can't bear the thought of another man touching you.'

Carol laughed bitterly. 'I really liked Roger and you've ruined it. Get out Graham. I should have done this a long time ago. It's over.'

Graham shook his head, but Carol was insistent. He left, head hanging, defeated.

Having managed to lose both his wife and lover within a matter of hours, Graham was gutted. He was surprised to discover that he felt worse about losing Marion than he had about Carol. He'd still be able to see Mel and would also support her, so that wasn't a problem. Being the practical man that he was, he knew he had to deal with his immediate concerns and find a place to stay for the weekend. Marion thought Graham had his own apartment but ever thrifty, for the last three years he had rented an en-suite room Monday to

Friday on the understanding that he'd be away every weekend. The rent was cheap and it gave him more money to maintain his double life, a lot of good that did him now he tutted. Margaret and Bernie were a kindly old couple and didn't bother him. He was at Carol's or working late most nights and only saw his landlord and landlady briefly before leaving for work each morning. There was no way Graham could return to his room this late on a Friday night. He toyed with the idea of contacting his sons but didn't fancy the drive to London and wasn't ready to explain that their mother was divorcing him. He assumed that Marion would eventually tell the twins about Carol and Mel and he didn't want to face that conversation with them until he had to. It was in this frame of mind that Graham booked into a Travelodge for the weekend. He entered the room and dropped his bag on the floor. He turned on the television and grabbed a plastic beaker from the bathroom. He poured a large measure of the half bottle of whisky into the cup and knocked it down in one, ignoring the raw burning sensation in his throat. He was drinking to forget and within an hour was spark out fully clothed on the bed, the whisky having done its job.

*****

Val felt like a zombie while taking the tablets. The doctor had prescribed tranquilisers and she'd used them as a crutch since the death of Ron and Ken. They didn't assuage the guilt but did stop her from bursting into tears randomly, whether in public or in private. She'd been off work sick. They said it was depression but Val knew that her guilt was to blame for everything she felt except for the grief. Mostly she couldn't tell the difference from the grief and the guilt, knowing that they both hurt like hell. She'd taken Ron for granted and missed him so much. She wondered how she could ever have fancied that idiot Ken. His death had been shocking but nothing to compare with how she'd felt

58

when the policeman had told her about Ron. It was all her fault and she knew that if she hadn't slept with Ken, Ron would still be alive and they could work out their problems. She would never have the opportunity to make things up to Ron now and that was something else to feel bad about. Val knew that she couldn't carry on with her life like this. She had to do something to make herself feel useful again. She hadn't taken the tablets for two days and the fuzziness was beginning to fade. The walls were closing in on her and she felt the urge to get out of the house.

Black clouds were rushing across the sky as if trying to win a race and the wind was whipping up the few leaves left from autumn into a frenzy. Val didn't notice as she walked to the bus stop, lost in her own dark thoughts. She didn't have long to wait and was soon sitting in the warm bus, the atmosphere muggy and dank from the moist air and other passengers. Arriving in town the rain had just started and Val stood on the pavement ignoring the people rushing around her and wondering what she should do. Shaking herself aware she decided to go into the Mall. At least she'd be dry wandering around aimlessly in there.

Two hours later she'd bought a scarf and gloves that she didn't really need, a hat for Libby and a new phone cover for Carl. She made her way up the escalator to browse in Debenhams. Looking at nothing in particular on the escalator going down she saw a face she recognised.

It was the mother of Claire, the girl who'd died with Ron, and she was sobbing. They hadn't met before, but Val recognized her face from the Memorial Service.

'Hello,' she called. 'Hello.' The people on the down escalator turned to stare at Val but Claire's mother kept facing forward, too absorbed in her own grief thought Val. She hurried to the top of the

59

escalator then ran back and made her way quickly down the other, her eyes following Marion all the while. She quickly caught up with her and tapped Marion on the shoulder. Marion turned, dabbing her eyes with a tissue. Val could see how upset she was and started crying herself.

'I'm Val,' she said between the tears. 'Ron's wife.' Marion's expression changed from confused to sympathetic and Val saw the effort it took for her to try and control herself.

Val took a breath and fought to control her own emotions. To say it had been heart breaking to lose her own husband was an understatement, but she couldn't imagine life without Carl or Libby. It was against all the laws of nature for parents to outlive their children yet this woman had lost a child and Val's heart went out to her, and for a moment she was able to put her own feelings to the back of her mind.

'Shall we go for a coffee?'

Marion nodded silently and Val led them to the coffee shop on the next corner. Now on a mission, Val grabbed a booth in the corner that had just been vacated. It gave them a bit of privacy and they could also people watch the shoppers if they wanted. The waitress took their order and Marion composed herself.

'I'm so embarrassed. I've learnt to control myself at home, but everything about London reminds me of Claire and the boys.' She explained that the twins had invited her down for the weekend.

'I told them their father's working away and can't get home this weekend.'

'I see,' said Val. It was obvious by her tone that Marion had lied to her sons and Val wondered why. She didn't have to wait long.

'I threw Graham out,' said Marion and Val nodded encouragement.

60

'I've known for years that he had another life and family but was willing to put up with it.'

The waitress came with the drinks and Val tried her best not to look shocked. Marion didn't look like the type who would put up with nonsense from anyone, never mind her husband. It just goes to show that you can't judge a book by its cover she thought.

'Then when we lost Claire, I didn't see the point any more. She always lived her life to the full just like my mother, and something changed in me.'

Losing her daughter must have been a lot to deal with, and now her marriage. Val's heart went out to Marion and she put a hand over hers.

'I'm so sorry,' was all she could manage but Marion seemed to appreciate the gesture.

'So your sons don't know?'

Marion shook her head. 'Not yet, no. I was hoping that their father would tell them but it's been two months and he still hasn't said anything. Tony and Jim aren't stupid and know something's going on,' she lifted her mug and took a sip of coffee. 'If Graham doesn't say anything soon I'll have to, but it should be him, especially as they've got a half-sister.'

'Oh, poor you, Marion. What are you going to do?'

'I really don't know. I feel the need to get away and do something useful. I can't stand the pain and sitting around thinking of Claire every day is slowly killing me.'

Something clicked with Val. Although their circumstances were different she'd found another lost soul who seemed to feel exactly the same as she did.

'I was having an affair when Ron died.' Val blurted it out and now it was Marion's turn to look shocked.

'Oh.' Val noticed her withdraw straight away and felt the need to explain.

'It was stupid and he wasn't half the man that my husband was. I'll regret it for the rest of my life and now Ron's gone and I can never tell him how sorry I am.' She started crying and Marion reached out to comfort her. She knew what it was like to be the wronged woman, but was determined not to judge Val. Nobody knew what went on inside a marriage except the married couple and though Val had made a mistake, Marion could see that it was now destroying her. Val stopped crying and looked at her new friend.

'He died of a heart attack the same night as Ron died. Ron dying was my punishment and I'll never forgive myself.'

Marion gasped.

'How tragic and how awful for you,' Marion squeezed her hand. 'You can't blame yourself, Val. It's a horrible coincidence yes, but not your fault.'

'But it must be. If I wasn't having an affair Ron wouldn't have been on night shift and would never have died, and neither would Ken.'

'It was their time, Val. They would have died that day whatever they'd been doing. That's the way it is. Not easy to hear or understand, but that's life I'm afraid. It wasn't your fault.' She smiled weakly.

'You really believe that? That there was nothing I could have done to prevent Ron's death, or Ken's? Ken wasn't half the man that Ron was and I don't know what I saw in him. I'm so sorry.' The last was said to herself.

'Listen, you can't change anything, Val. You need to try and move on.' Marion knew that she should take her own advice but for the moment, felt an overwhelming need to comfort her new friend.

The irony wasn't lost on Val.

'Talk about the blind leading the blind,' said Val.

They looked out of the window as a person dressed as a clown walked by. The clown seemed out of place among the casually dressed shoppers in the Mall and the women did a double take and looked at each other, the bizarre sight lightening their mood. Marion's eyes twinkled and her smile turned into a giggle. Val chuckled and both women erupted into fits of laughter, releasing the tension of the previous months. Other patrons looked toward the booth in the corner and when Marion stood to make her way to the toilets, were surprised to see a middle-aged woman and not a youngster.

They both felt better for crying, laughing and talking and sat in comfortable silence for a few minutes on Marion's return. An idea had been forming in Val's head and she decided to run it by her new friend. At worst she would say no, but there was a chance that she might go along with it.

'Marion?'

'Yes.'

'You know you said you want to get away and do something?'

Marion leaned forward, curious.

'Well, have you heard of the charity People Against Poverty?'

'Hasn't everyone?' Marion had seen the TV adverts requesting funds, the mental images of the poor children that had disappeared because of her own personal grief, now returned.

'Well,' said Val. 'Would you consider working for them?'

'I haven't really thought about doing something like that.'

'We could maybe do it together. Doing something for charity would make me feel better about myself and I would be happier if I had company. You

63

seem to be at a loose end and we could really make a difference...'

Val stopped, and wondered if she'd made a mistake. Marion seemed to be looking at something in the far distance and Val wasn't sure whether she was still paying attention. She couldn't wait any longer.

'Well?'

'Do you know,' Marion smiled. 'That might just be the saving of me. When do we start?'

They chatted for a little longer about their families, the unfairness of life, but mostly about the opportunities ahead. The time flew and when the waitress asked if they'd like to order food they decided it was time to leave. They swapped telephone numbers and email addresses and Val said she'd do further research and let Marion know the outcome.

'I'm not going to say anything to my children until I know whether we'll be accepted,' said Val, and Marion agreed that was a good idea. After an awkward hug, they departed in different directions, each woman with a new sense of purpose and a spring in her step.

Strike when the iron's hot thought Val as she picked up the phone to dial the charity some time later. She knew that if she didn't do it now she might lose her bottle. After a nerve-wracking but pleasant conversation, she hung up and called Marion with the news that their initial interviews, by telephone, had been scheduled for the following Tuesday. The woman had explained that subject to passing the phone interview and a police and criminal records check they could expect to be loaded onto a course within the next few months.

*****

Val was waiting for Carl and Libby to arrive and Ron awaited the arrival of his children with almost as much enthusiasm and anticipation as his wife. He hadn't seen them since his funeral and was keen to see how they were getting on. Carl was studying Computer Science at Edinburgh University and although Ron was inordinately proud of his son, he had missed their Sunday afternoons together for the past three years. It was just as well that Carl was undertaking a project in London and had travelled down the previous night otherwise Val would have had to give him her news, whatever that was, over the phone. Libby, studying History and English at London University lived on the other side of the city and, Ron assumed, was coming home for the weekend.

They met outside on the pavement approaching each other from opposite directions. Libby hadn't seen her younger brother since their father's funeral and seeing him now reminded her of that awful day. They hugged for a long time until Libby stopped crying. She dried her eyes and did her best to look cheerful. She didn't want her mother to see how upset she was in case it started her off. Carl gave his sister a gentle push and she walked up the concrete steps to the house followed by her brother.

Val had watched her children hugging and her daughter crying and was in floods of tears when she opened the front door, so Libby's efforts had been to no avail. Carl quickly excused himself and made his way to the kitchen to make the coffee.

That's my boy thought Ron smiling to himself. Carl was exactly like he was, beating a hasty retreat as soon as the women became emotional, or wanted to talk about their feelings. Carl returned to the lounge and Ron could see that Val was ready to impart her news.

'I know you were both worried about me taking tranquilisers.' Her children nodded. 'You'll be glad to know that I've stopped them and so far so good, touch

65

wood.' She tapped the table with her forefinger and looked up, brandishing a big smile.

Both glad to see their mother starting to look well again, Libby knew there'd been other changes. She hadn't seen her mother for a few weeks and she sensed an air of optimism compared to the last time she'd been home when the house seemed to have been mired in a fog of gloom and doom. Although this was understandable Libby had still been relieved to return to the norm of university.

'What's happened?'

'I've enrolled on a course.'

'Oh, well done, Mum. Good for you. When do you start?'

'Second week in January.'

'That's great. Which night?' said Carl, assuming that his mother was going to evening classes.

'It's a full-time course, Carl. On the outskirts of the city and I'll be staying in a hotel.'

'Oh, right. How long?' Carl wasn't sure how he felt about his mother going away for a course so wanted to hear more.

'It's only a week.' She smiled again and Libby just knew there was more to this than met the eye.

'Well good for you,' said Carl and Val waited for the pat on her head.

'Right, Mother, spill. The whole story.'

Val knew her daughter would pick-up the good news vibes. Well, her good news anyway. 'The course is also a suitability test, and if I pass...' she took a sip of coffee and picked up a biscuit deliberately keeping them in suspense and enjoying their anticipation.

'Mother!' said Carl, his patience wearing thin.

'Have you heard of *People Against Poverty*?'

They both nodded. Always on the scrounge for other people's well-earned cash, thought Carl unkindly.

'Well, if they like me and I like them, I'm off to Zambia to work for them as a volunteer. Food and board's included of course.'

'But you can't,' said Carl, 'it's in Africa and too dangerous.'

Val sighed. 'It's not a war zone, Carl. I'll be perfectly fine and I'll be with a friend.'

'I'm well aware it's not a war zone, Mother, thank you,' he harrumphed, exasperated. 'They have malaria and other such diseases that we don't have in this country.'

'And I'm well aware of that, thank you, Carl,' she adored her son but he could be damned patronizing at times. 'I've already had the necessary inoculations in case I'm successful, you'll be pleased to hear, and before you say it,' Val raised a hand at her son to stop him interrupting. 'I'll come to no harm from having them.'

Libby knew that for some reason her mother felt guilty about her father's death. She also knew that this course and new career would do her the world of good. She could see where the conversation was going, they were so alike and often butted heads. As usual when her brother and mother were at loggerheads she played the role of mediator.

'Good for you, Mum. I think it's a great idea. And who's the friend?'

Carl interrupted before his mother had a chance to respond. 'You aren't serious, surely?' He was in a strop now and Libby could see that logic wouldn't convince him.

'Carl, we have our lives ahead of us. We've lost our father but Mum's lost her lifelong partner. Cut her some slack, please.'

Val couldn't cope with an argument with Carl and sank into the settee, huge sobs wracking her entire body.

Carl rushed to her side and held her until the sobs subsided.

'I'm sorry, Mum. It's only because we worry about you.' Val nodded in between the sobs.

'It's only for three months, and then I'll decide what to do after that.'

'When will you go?'

'February if we pass the course.' Now back in control of her emotions, she continued. 'Will you come and look after the house while I'm away, Libby? You can bring a friend to keep you company.'

'Of course,' said Libby, 'and who's the friend going with you?'

'Marion Sylvester,' said Val. The name didn't ring any bells with Carl, but Libby knew she'd heard the surname before but the only one she could think of was the girl who'd died in her father's taxi. She said as much to her mother.

'That's right. It is Claire's mother.'

Both her children looked at her and wondered whether she had lost the plot.

'I'll be able to come home for Christmas after all,' was the best that Carl could manage as he planned to tell his mates he wouldn't be going away with them that year.

Carl wasn't the only one who was concerned. Ron wasn't happy that Val was doing a course then going away, it was far too soon after his death as far as he was concerned, and she was still vulnerable. He'd been able to move Jay's tablet bottle when he was with Claire and when he'd heard Val's news had tried his best to cause a spiritual stir, to make them aware of his presence. He'd blown to create a breeze, had tried moving items by thought and had generally made as much noise as was possible in his current state. All to no effect. Ron shook his fists in frustration still shouting at

Val not to go, even though he knew it was pointless. He'd need to find Claire and get her to assist him. If she refused, he would do his best to make her visits to the living world as difficult as possible.

Chapter 5

Ron had been calling for Claire on and off for days. He needed her help and was impatient to visit his family again.

'Ah, you're back,' he said. 'For a minute there I thought I'd lost you for good.'

'How long have I been out of it?' Claire stretched and yawned like a lazy lion.

'Couple of months at least. After a while I was worried so kept calling Gabriella to find out what was going on.'

'I thought she was too busy to, um, visit.'

'She is.' Ron chuckled. 'After I got bored with my own company I kept shouting and she came and gave me a bollocking. Told me I was driving her nuts but answered a few questions anyway, before disappearing again.'

'And?'

'Well, apparently you are one of the few who can contact people through dreams, so soon after your own death. It normally takes at least two years, and even then not everyone is able to do it.'

'Aren't I the clever one?'

Ron shook his head at her smugness.

'The downside, as you will have gathered, is that it takes a lot out of you. So use your gift wisely.'

'Yes, Obi Wan,' said Claire and they both doubled up, laughing like they were alive again.

When they'd laughed themselves out, Ron turned serious.

'I need your help. Val's about to do a course then go to Zambia and I don't want her to go.' He explained about the visit to his family while Claire had been sleeping.

'But I want to see how mine are getting on first,' she said, falsely confident and wondering how she'd react to seeing the people she loved carrying on with their lives without her.

'Well I can tell you how your mother's getting on. She's going on the same course as Val and is going to work for the same charity.'

'It's even more important that I catch up with them then. What about my father, what does he have to say about it?'

'Claire, we don't have much time if I want to stop her from going. Can we do this first, please?'

It was obvious how desperate Ron was so Claire reluctantly capitulated and they were in Val's house in no time.

It was the period between Christmas and the New Year. The first Christmas without her husband and their father had been dreadful for them all. Val had tried to make it jolly and had overcompensated by buying Carl and Libby lots of presents, going over the top with the decorations and too much food and drink. They'd braved Christmas Day, falsely. All three had pretended to enjoy themselves. Val recalled that it had been about 4 o'clock when Libby looked at the uneaten food and said that she couldn't cope any more. She ran upstairs in tears. She'd re-joined her mother and brother later and opened a bottle of wine. Carl had taken that as an escape signal and had gone to visit an old school friend, assuring his mother that it hadn't been pre-arranged. Val and Libby had drunk until they both fell asleep watching an old movie. They weren't actively watching it she recalled, but it had been on and it avoided the need to talk. Christmas time had heightened their loss and they were both on an emotional precipice, neither wanting to fall into the abyss below. It had been an unpleasant day that had

71

lasted too long for Val's liking. She hoped that next year the kids would spend the day with their friends or partners – if they had them by then – and she could sneak off and help those in greater need. She knew it was selfish but being busy would be less painful, and take her mind off the wonderful family Christmases that were now in the dim and distant past.

Val stood up and shook herself. Her line dancing friends had invited her out on New Year's Eve. She used to go twice a week, religiously, but hadn't been since Ron's death. It was good of them all to remember her and Val was looking forward to catching up. It would soon be the New Year and Val thought she'd better start sorting out the stuff for her course and also the clothes she'd need for Zambia should she and Marion be successful. Best to be optimistic because if this didn't come off, Val didn't know what she was going to do with the rest of her life.

'Now, Claire,' said Ron. 'I'll count to three then we'll blow my photo off the mantelpiece. She's bound to see that as a sign. Okay?' Ron sounded determined but Claire wasn't sure this was a good plan.

'Don't you think it'll scare her?'

'She wasn't frightened of me when I was alive, so why would she be when I'm dead?'

That wasn't quite how Claire saw it, but she could tell by his tone that she wouldn't be able to talk him out of it. She reluctantly agreed and psyched herself up for the task.

'Ready?'

Claire nodded.

'One, two, three.' They blew as hard as they could and nothing happened. Val left the room and jogged up the stairs to her bedroom.

'What happened? Why didn't it move?' Ron could see that Claire had exerted as much effort as he had.

'I really don't know, because that was exhausting.'

Not one to give up, Ron insisted they keep trying. They followed Val around for most of that day, unsuccessfully attempting to knock over or move various items. By the time Val retired for the night, both spirits were spent and they returned to Cherussola, trying to figure out why they'd been able to move Jay's tablet bottle, but nothing belonging to Val.

Claire was resting after their tiring day and on her way to oblivion while thinking pleasant thoughts of Jay. Since his botched overdose attempt she knew he'd suffered for being unfaithful and had now forgiven him for it.

'I've got it!' Shouted Ron and Claire jumped in fright.

'Bloody hell, you scared the life out of me.' Ron's look was a question.

'Yes, I know I'm already dead, but it's only a figure of speech.' She sighed.

Ignoring her remark, he was eager to share his theory. 'Maybe it's only if someone is in trouble. Jay was on the verge of taking his own life so we were able to stop him. We have to find people in trouble or danger and then see if it works. What do you think?'

Claire had no idea if Ron's theory was correct. She did know that she couldn't attempt anything until she was properly rested and revived.

'We can certainly give it a go, Ron.'

'Come on…'

'To know whether it works we have to have all out strength so I'm sorry, but it's going to have to wait.'

He knew she was right so they both relaxed lost in their own thoughts until taken to the strange

73

Cherussola world where dead people rest, but not in their final resting place.

*****

She didn't know how much later it was when she opened her eyes. Ron wasn't about so Claire decided to visit her own family, before he reappeared and tried to put his needs first.

Marion knew that Val had told her children their news before Christmas, but as Graham had not yet told the boys about his other family, she knew this task fell to her. She decided to wait until the New Year, rather than make Christmas even worse for all of them. The twins said they'd be home for Christmas and Marion had lied to them and told them that their parents would be spending Christmas with friends, as they couldn't bear to be in the house at Christmas with only memories of Claire. This hadn't seemed right to the twins and when they tried to speak to their father during the Christmas break, their mother told them that he was busy or had returned to work early. The twins had now been summoned to Yorkshire at their mother's request.

'I don't know why she wants to see us,' said Jim, answering his brother's unasked question. Others including their long-standing friends often thought their telepathy was weird, but they'd had the uncanny ability to read each other's minds since they were very young, and neither found it strange.

Tony parked in the driveway and looked at his brother. 'Me too,' he said as he opened the door, knowing that Jim also had a bad feeling about the visit.

Although their lives would never be the same without Claire, they had all tried to settle back into some sort of routine during the six months since her

74

death. The way the twins had coped was to immerse themselves in their work and sport when they weren't working. Between that and finding time to see their girlfriends, they didn't see their parents as often as they wanted. They made a point of calling their mother every week but important issues were never discussed and she always said that she was doing okay. The twins were therefore surprised to see that their mother had lost weight and dyed her hair. She'd also had the house decorated and it looked more modern than it had before. There was an air of *new woman* about her and the twins felt that she'd turned a corner and was trying to get on with her life.

'You look great, Mum,' said Tony, and Jim nodded in agreement. They kissed and Marion brought the boys tea and sandwiches. They were surprised that cups and saucers had been dispensed with and replaced with mugs and gave each other a questioning look.

'The house looks brill too,' said Jim. 'What does Dad think about it all?'

'That's one of the things I want to talk to you about.'

Both sons knew they weren't going to like her explanation.

'When did you last speak to your father?' asked Marion as she raised her cup to her lips. Her sons were comforted by the fact that their mother still used a cup and saucer.

'We speak to him during the week, Mum, the same as you,' said Jim.

'Why are you asking? He must have told you,' Tony added and looked at his brother. They spoke to both parents during the week and knew they had each other for company at the weekends so left them to their own devices.

Marion sighed and returned her cup and saucer to the table. She joined her hands together in

75

her lap and leaned forward. Sensing a bombshell, her sons nervously awaited her news.

'There's no easy way to tell you this.'

'For Christ's sake, Mum. Just spit it out would you? You're driving us nuts,' Tony blurted and his brother nodded.

'Your father and I are in the process of getting divorced.'

'Oh, right.' Tony calmed down and felt his pulse steadying. They had both thought that one of their parents may be terminally ill so although the news wasn't good, it was better than anticipated. They also knew that sometimes the death of a child could either make a marriage stronger or break it apart, so although sad, they both breathed a sigh of relief.

Jim walked to his mother's chair and sat on the arm. He lifted her hand and held it. 'I'm sorry, Mum, it must be awful for both of you. If you need anything...'

'That's not all of it,' she interrupted and took back her hand. Marion was trying to find the right way to tell her sons about their father's double life and she stalled, lifting her tea and taking another sip. The twins waited trying to be patient but their pulses started racing once again.

'Please, Mum?' said Jim. 'Just take your time and tell us what's going on.'

'Your father,' she looked at each of them in turn. 'Your loving, bastard father...'

Both sons sucked in air at their mother's use of a word they would never have imagined her using. It would be like the Pope telling someone to fuck off thought Tony.

'...has been leading a double-life for at least fifteen years.'

Marion sat back nodding, and waited for a response.

'What, he's a spy or something?'

76

'Don't be stupid, Jim. He's not a bloody spy. He has another family.'

'What!' said in unison. The twins looked at their mother as if she were from another planet.

When they calmed down and stopped firing questions at her Marion explained.

'I hired a private investigator and discovered that your bastard father has been having a long-term relationship with a woman named Carol. And they have a daughter who's nearly fifteen, named Mel.'

The twins were initially dumbstruck. When the information sank in, they were annoyed and also curious.

'I can't answer your questions and I only know what the private investigator has told me about your half-sister, which I've already shared with you.' She folded her hands together again in her lap. 'I'm sorry your bastard father has been cowardly and hasn't told you.'

Although Tony was preoccupied with his mother's new title for his father, it sounded to Jim as if his mother was still holding something back.

'When did you and Dad split up?'

'Does it matter, Jim? I've told you what I know and it's your bastard father who's in the wrong here. You should be grilling him and not me.'

They looked at each other and Marion sensed that they were sharing thoughts as they often did. She waited for Tony to ask the next question.

'How long have you known and when did you break up, Mum?' He folded his arms and eyed his mother suspiciously.

'I'm not on trial here, and as I said, you need to speak to your bastard father. Now if you'll excuse me,' she looked at her watch, 'I have a train to catch and you can either give me a lift to the station or I'll get a taxi. I'm not bothered either way.'

The twins had expected to stay overnight. They didn't want their mother to be agitated more than she already was, so didn't argue when she requested a lift on the condition that they wouldn't ask further questions about the disintegration of their parents' marriage, or their newly discovered half-sister. On the way to the station there was another revelation, surprising but less shocking.

'Where are you off to, Mum?' asked Tony, trying to lighten the mood.

'I'm going on a course. Your sister always said there was more to life than Yorkshire and that I should travel more, so that's what I'm doing.' With the drama of the revelations, it was the first time that afternoon that Claire had been mentioned and Marion wiped a few tears from her eyes. It was still massively raw and painful but she was trying her best to think and speak about Claire without sobbing her heart out each time. Sometimes she succeeded, others not. She wouldn't wish this pain on her worst enemy and on some of the dark lonely nights had wondered how she could possibly carry on with the rest of her life.

'On your own?' Tony's voice brought her back to the present.

'No. Val Wilkinson, the widow of the taxi driver who killed your sister talked me into doing it.'

The boys remained quiet, wondering what this woman had done with their real mother.

'The course is with *People Against Poverty* and if we pass it, we're off to Zambia for three months.'

'What!' shouted her sons.

'That'll show your bastard father,' said Marion, as if she hadn't heard them.

They travelled the rest of the way in silence. Marion looking forward to her new adventure, and the twins furious with their father, curious about their new half-sister, and not sure what to think about their mother's new career.

*****

Claire was as shocked as her brothers at her mother's revelation. Ron was nowhere to be found so she had time to think. Her father had been having an affair and had fathered a child who was nearly 15 years old. So she had a half-sister who she would never meet. Not that she felt she wanted to meet her at the moment, but she'd had the choice taken away from her. And he had another woman on the go. How could he do that to her mother and how could he deceive her and the twins? Claire was once again furious and hadn't calmed down by the time Ron arrived.

'What's up?' he asked and she explained. He could see she was hurt and angry and felt sorry for the lass. Since dying she'd discovered about her fiancé's indiscretion with her best friend, and now, that her father had deceived her whole family as well. It would take a long time for Claire to get over her father's betrayal and he felt she needed to be busy.

'Do you want to go and see your father?' Claire felt Ron's arm around her and she leant into his shoulder as the tears ran down her face, the anger now dissipated.

'He's the last person I want to see at the moment.' She laughed bitterly. 'The more I think about it the more a lot of things seem to make sense.' Ron moved a hair from Claire's eye and nodded encouragement.

'I remember Mum being confused when one of Dad's team told her that he'd had a chance of a job near home and he'd turned it down,' she hesitated, trying to control the tears. 'Dad said that it was a rumour and that the fella didn't know what he was talking about, but it didn't ring true at the time.'

79

Ron held Claire and remained silent. He knew she'd work things out in her own time and eventually come to terms with this new turn of events.

'Look, Ron!' she shouted shattering the mood.

'What, what is it?'

'I'm crying, real tears.' He looked and she was. Although they'd felt as if they'd cried since dying, there hadn't been any physical evidence. But now they looked down and as well as the tears, they appeared to have proper bodies again.

'Does this mean that people will see us when we go to Earth?' Claire shrugged.

'No, I don't know either. Shall we go and have a look?'

*****

Claire recognized the London underground as soon as they arrived. She wasn't sure of the station but knew it wasn't rush hour. There were a number of tourists on the platform but no business people or bored looking commuters waiting to resume their tedious journeys to their tedious little jobs, that Claire would have given anything for at that moment. She corrected herself. There was one businessman dressed in a snazzy suit who looked out of place among the collection of tourists. She heard the *mind the gap* announcement and knew that a train must be approaching. Ron pointed in the direction of the suited man who started walking quickly to the platform's edge - too quickly. They both knew exactly what he planned to do.

'Now!' shouted Ron. They attempted to combine their thoughts and strength, Claire frowning with concentration in her efforts to keep the man on the platform. The events seemed to move in slow motion for Claire, Ron and the passengers on the platform, as the man jumped and the train hit him. It was as if he had the body of a rag doll as the momentum of the train flew it along the track, before it disappeared under the carriages. The spirits saw his soul leave his body and hover in the air. His soul looked terrified first of all as ugly hands grabbed at it from below trying to pull it in their direction. They were soon outnumbered by gentle caressing hands which eventually prevailed and the dead man's soul travelled upwards, now looking at his human shell in confusion, as if he couldn't believe he'd actually done the deed.

Pandemonium broke out on the platform as a woman screamed and other passengers looked on in horror, then disgust as a man complained about the delay the suicide victim had caused. Police and paramedics arrived in record time and the shocked driver was helped from his cabin and taken away by colleagues.

Even knowing what they now knew about death, Claire and Ron were still upset.

'The poor soul must have been tormented to end his own life like that,' said Ron. Claire nodded. 'How awful for his family and why couldn't we do anything?' It was a question neither could answer and they were frustrated at not being able to help.

'I thought I was meant to have special powers.'

'Maybe it was his time,' said Ron and they left the scene, not noticing one woman who had turned very white and was standing still, staring at the space they'd vacated.

Chapter 6

Ron and Claire were on one of their visits as opposed to watching from their new home.

'Are you ready to go and see your father yet?' Claire thought about it. She adored her father but was still annoyed about his deceit.

'I know the best way ahead is to discover his side of the story as well, Ron, but I'm still so angry with him and afraid I'd do something I might regret if I went to see him now. I know my brothers must feel the same too, as they haven't been to see him yet.'

Ron didn't know her brothers so didn't comment. He couldn't imagine what Claire would do to her father but did understand her anger.

'Okay, we'll leave it for a while,' he smiled sympathetically, 'but only if you're sure?'

Claire was trying to be more mature and forgiving in her outlook and re-thought her decision.

'Come on then. I'm ready to visit my father but I warn you, I'll probably get emotional.'

Talk about stating the obvious. 'No problem, Claire. I can handle it.'

*****

Graham had faced the sack or a visit to the doctor. He'd chosen the latter and had been signed off for six weeks having been told he was suffering from depression. He'd been prescribed tablets and the doctor had also advised him to get some exercise and lose weight. He'd moved into his current flat the weekend after his relationships had fallen apart and he looked around now at the boxes still packed in the corner of the room. He was too ashamed and frightened to speak to his sons. Marion and Carol had made it perfectly clear that they never wanted to see him again and Mel had refused to speak to him since he'd broken up with her mother. Graham picked up the plate and looked at the cakes, the only comfort in his sad miserable life. Whether to have a chocolate éclair, apple turnover or jam donut was the biggest decision he would make today. What the hell, he thought as he selected the giant éclair. It made no difference which one he ate now as they'd all be gone within the hour. He switched on the TV and surfed channels. A gardening programme and chat show later, Graham put the empty plate down next to him on the sofa and looked at the sad crumbs. He turned his head upwards, his face a mask of misery.

'Claire, Claire, Claire!' he cried out. 'Oh Claire. What have I done? WHAT HAVE I DONE?' Graham picked up the plate and threw it at the television, watching in wonder as the plate and the screen smashed into smithereens. He bent forward, put his head in his hands and cried. It was the first time that Graham had cried in years. He cried for the loss of his marriage, his relationship with Carol, in self-pity, in shame, but most of all for the loss of his beautiful daughter who he hadn't seen enough when she was alive and now missed like hell. He sobbed his heart out like a young child until he was totally spent, then he curled up on the sofa hugging his knees to his chest and for the first time in months slept a dreamless sleep.

The anger that Claire had felt since she'd discovered her father's double life drained from her as if someone had opened the floodgates. She was overcome with love for the fat man that she hardly recognized and knew he was in dire need of help. As she had with Jay, Claire tried to visit her father in his sleep. Even as she tried she knew she wasn't getting through. Ron had silently watched the whole sorry episode and when he could see that Claire was no longer concentrating suggested that it was time to leave.

'We can't do anything for him at the moment. You'll only upset yourself more if we stay.'

She was reluctant to leave.

'Come on, Claire.' Ron tried pulling her but she shook him off. 'Let's go back where there's no distractions and think about what we can do for him.'

Claire must have agreed without consciously thinking about it as she opened her eyes and they were back in Cherussola. In the land of Cherussola thought Claire as she collapsed on the clean cream leather sofa that was the most comfortable she'd ever sat on.

'Look at this, Ron.' She couldn't shake the image of her father from her mind but that didn't stop her from being impressed with the new addition to their so called home.

'We must have started thinking about home comforts without realizing that we were doing so.'

'Let's think up a few more things then.' They both concentrated but nothing appeared despite their best efforts.

'On second thoughts, perhaps you only get things that you don't ask for.'

Ron agreed and thought about their situation. It was strange, they never felt hungry but didn't eat, never smelt dirty but didn't wash, and their clothes were always clean. Claire hadn't changed clothes since she'd died but when she remembered to look was always dressed in something different. They felt the whole range of human emotions and were also able to use all their senses while there, but some of these senses were ineffective back on the living plain. They also felt extremely tired following visits to Earth, the degree of tiredness dependent on what they had or hadn't done. Sometimes Claire was out of action for months after such visits but she felt a little less tired each time and likened it to some sort of acclimatisation.

'Wonder how it all works?' she asked and Ron shrugged. He wasn't one for spending time on riddles he couldn't solve.

'Anyway, Ron, enough of this pontificating. We have work to do.' He didn't point out that it was her who had been pontificating and waited for her next brainwave.

Claire could see he wasn't going to bite, so continued. 'My father needs help and I can't give it to him. But I know two men that can. Come on.'

Ron accompanied her without argument and they made their way back to the land of the living.

*****

It was the twins' football night and they'd decided to have a drink after the match and then return to the flat. Tony and his girlfriend had recently split so Jim and Fiona had decided not to see each other every night, so that Jim could hang out with Tony. They retired early to bed with aching muscles but happily tired after their win and friendly banter with the other lads. Jim noticed the dark circles under his brother's eyes as he grabbed a quick coffee before work the following morning.

'Still thinking about Hannah?'

'Nope. Claire and Dad actually,' Tony took a sip of coffee. 'Dreamed of both of them last night.'

'No shit,' said Jim. 'What happened in your dream?'

Tony could see that his brother was fishing and guessed straight away.

'You too eh?' Jim nodded. So they'd both dreamt that Claire had told them their father was in a bad way and that they should visit him.

'It's understandable after all that's happened,' said Jim. 'but I'm still too angry with him and I'd just lose it.'

'And me but aren't you curious about our half-sister? I know I am.'

'I am but it would somehow feel like a betrayal to Claire and I wouldn't want to meet her feeling like that. Shall we give it a bit more time?'

'Yup, sounds like a plan,' said Tony, putting on his coat, 'see you later.'

'Damn, damn, damn,' Claire shouted at Ron. 'They're so bloody stubborn at times.' Family trait, thought Ron but chose not to comment.

'You can't force them into doing something they don't want to, Claire.'

'I could when I was alive, so watch this space.' She was determined that she would convince her brothers to visit her father sooner rather than later.

In a hurry that morning, Tony hadn't had time for his usual routine before leaving the flat. He picked up a newspaper from a colleague's desk and made his way to the facilities. Leisurely studying page three while answering the call of nature, a gust blew into the cubicle and he had to fold the newspaper to stop it from blowing away. Someone must have opened a window earlier, thought Tony, but the weather had been calm when he was travelling to work and he hadn't heard anything about a storm brewing. He opened the paper again but as soon as he did so, an image of his sister appeared in his mind's eye, it seemed so real to Tony that he gasped.

'Claire?'

'Visit Dad, he needs you,' was all she said.

'Bloody hell, Claire! I'm on the loo for God's sake.'

He heard his sister's giggle which was followed by a small gust of wind, then absolute silence. Tony hastily finished what he was doing and left the cubicle. He looked at his pale face in the mirror and splashed cold water over it after washing his hands. This was no dream and he took a moment to come to terms with what had happened. He thought that he'd be spooked. He was shocked but not frightened. He'd adored Claire but when she wanted something she could be a right pain in the arse. Apparently this was the case whether she was alive or dead. Tony laughed to himself as he left the company bathroom, his sister's visit had actually given him some comfort and he knew that he wouldn't get any peace until they went to see their father. Returning to his office he picked up his phone to call his brother, and wondered how she'd got her message across to him.

'Same here,' said Jim when he answered the phone. 'But I was in a meeting with the boss. He asked me a question. I was forming my answer and she appeared in my head, telling me that Dad needs me. The boss must have thought I was losing my mind when I said, *You're supposed to be dead.* I excused myself quickly and she was laughing. Why couldn't she have waited?'

Claire managed to stay with it as she watched the twins speak as if a visit from their dead sister was a completely natural occurrence. It had worked and she knew that they'd find the time to visit their father, probably that weekend.

Ron had watched in amazement. They hadn't been able to contact anyone since the episode with Jay, and now Claire had visited both her brothers simply because she had wanted to. He could see that it had totally drained her but he needed answers.

'What were you thinking? How did you do it? Can you do it again?'

Claire put up a hand. 'Tired, Ron. Need to rest.'

They were back on the cream sofa and she lay down and closed her eyes. 'Later.' She faded as she spoke the last word and Ron knew he'd have to wait for his answers, possibly for quite a while.

As Claire drifted away her wedding fantasy appeared and she smiled. This time Tash was no longer a bridesmaid and had been replaced by Mel. Although Claire had forgiven her, she didn't want to be reminded of her friend's deceit on her wedding day. Her half-sister was a vague version of what she imagined her to be, but plumper than the real Mel as Claire remembered immodestly how good she had looked at age fifteen and didn't want her young sister to upstage her on her special day. The ceremony continued until Claire was too exhausted to think any longer.

Chapter 7

The night before the course was due to start, both Val and Marion were happier than they'd been since the accident. A purpose had returned to their lives and they were like twenty-somethings at the beginning of a weekend. Marion looked around the room they were sharing.

'London's not exactly cheap is it? Wonder how much this hotel costs the charity?' She had expected more frugal accommodation. They each had a queen size bed and a separate wardrobe. There was one desk and chair and at the other side of the room, and a sofa was positioned against the far wall facing a TV screen. The bathroom contained both a bath and separate shower with toilet and bidet.

Val explained that a rich benefactor had left the hotel to the charity, and that they made money out of it by running it as a going concern.

'Having the courses outside of the summer tourist season and carrying out the training in the conference facility saves them from paying out money. That's why we're with this lot, because they don't waste much money on administration and stuff.'

'Fair point,' Marion was impressed that Val had done her homework. 'Shall we eat?' They made their way to the hotel's restaurant and enjoyed a delicious dinner while discussing the course programme.

They felt refreshed and were raring to go the following morning as they met the other students over coffee in the conference anteroom. In total there were five women and six men who hoped to work for the charity. Most were in their twenties and thirties with the exception of Val and Marion and a married couple who had retired, had travelled large parts of the world, and were now looking for a new adventure and wanted to give something back to society.

A short thirty-something lady hurried into the room. She got their attention without asking.

'Hi everyone, I'm Gail and I'll be taking you through the programme this week. Ready to make a start?'

She was one of those people who made everyone feel special and when Marion looked around the room, they were all smiling at Gail. Marion liked her instantly and joined the others as they followed her into the conference room. She couldn't sit next to Val as the old married couple had already seated themselves either side of her. She gave Val a look and sat directly opposite.

'Happy where you are?' asked Gail after looking around and picking up on the body language. Everyone nodded, content, or at least pretending to be.

Gail stood up and put both hands on the table in front of her.

'As I said, my name's Gail and I'll run through the course programme first.' She explained that the five days would include information on volunteering, their charity, suitability assessments and the final two days when the groups would be split into their own project areas and learn about their particular area or country. They'd re-join for two hours on the Friday afternoon for a post course discussion and review.

'But first,' she said. 'I'm going to tell you a bit about me. I come from a broken home and had a difficult childhood. I'm happy and sorted now but it's taken a while for me to get to where I am today.' She sat down and surveyed her class. 'That's still hard for me to do but I'll make it easier for you guys.' They smiled nervously and Marion figured that they were all in the same boat. 'I'm going to split you into three threes and one two. Tell the other people or person in your group about yourselves and when you've finished your discussions, I want you to tell the whole class about the other people in your group.'

Val was grouped with Mr and Mrs Fox and they kept interrupting each other. They loved to talk and she was quite happy not having to tell her life story, especially the events of the last year. The plan had been for Val and Marion to be together but as they were discovering, events very rarely went to plan.

Marion tried to gain Val's attention but it didn't work. At first Marion was happy that Dylan and Joanne, the other two within her group, were getting on so well. It became tedious after a while and Marion totally switched off, but not before she had discovered enough about the youngsters to answer any number of questions. When it came to their group Joanne was able to relay Dylan's life so far to the rest of the class. Marion did a good job of telling the group all about Joanne but, as she expected, Dylan had a problem telling them anything other than the basics about her. Gail let him squirm for a minute or so then to save him further embarrassment, asked Marion to tell them all about herself. She kept it as brief as possible. As she'd discussed with Val the previous evening, and not wanting pity or sympathy, Marion left out the detail about Claire and her own divorce. Val did the same about Ron and sensed that Gail knew she was holding back. Gail had been a trainer for five years and had met all sorts of people. She knew that not everyone was comfortable sharing the most intimate details of their lives and didn't push it. All of them had volunteered for the particular projects and would be paid expenses and the food and accommodation provided for them. They were willing to give up their time and as long as they were decent and law abiding people, Gail wasn't bothered if there were any skeletons in their closets.

The course progressed and the students became closer and enjoyed the usual banter that occurs when a number of people share the same classroom for more than one day. They were split into their project groups on the Thursday. Most lived in the city so they agreed to get together on the Friday for post course discussions and drinks. Val had invited Marion to stay for the weekend and she'd agreed enthusiastically.

Marion already had a buyer for their house in Yorkshire and wanted to find a flat in London. The mortgage payments had been too much and Graham didn't want to live there or buy her out – according to her solicitor – so she really hadn't had much choice. She had a few close friends in Yorkshire but no family and really felt the need for a fresh start. She'd told the twins and they were happy she was moving to the city, though sad that the home where they'd grown up with their sister was being sold. She didn't expect to see much of her sons as she'd already decided that if she enjoyed the volunteer work abroad, she would try to stay in the charity sector and get a paid job.

In the hotel bar they all agreed that it had been an enjoyable and worthwhile course. The Foxes were the only ones going to Zambia with Marion and Val and they all talked enthusiastically about the new project. The remaining seven were off to Vietnam so the groups had plenty to discuss and Gail also joined them for a few drinks before leaving for home.

'You've been a great course,' she smiled. 'Have you all enjoyed it?'

'Bet you say that to everyone.' Gail gave Dylan a knowing smile and tapped the side of her nose. She said goodbye and after they thanked her there was a lull in the conversation.

'Anyone fancy painting the town red?' asked Joanne and the Foxes and Marion declined. Val put her hands out, palms up and shrugged at Marion.

'Sorry, Val but I think I'm coming down with something and I've got stuff to do this weekend too.'

'Like?'

Everyone waited for the answer but Marion wanted to speak to her sons before sharing the news with Val. Used to keeping her private life to herself she didn't want her course companions to know her circumstances so was suitably evasive.

'I'll let you know later, or maybe tomorrow would be better.'

Val nodded. They would leave the hotel the following morning and travel to her house. Val wondered if she should stay and keep Marion company and she pulled her to one side.

'Do you want me to stay and we'll buy some wine and take it to the room?'

Marion knew she was asking purely out of politeness. 'No really, Val, you go out. I don't feel like drinking tonight anyway. I'm hoping that if I have an early night I'll feel better in the morning and this,' she sniffed, 'won't develop into anything worse.'

'Oh, okay. I hope you feel better soon and I'll try not to make too much noise when I return.'

Marion said her goodbyes to Val and the youngsters. The Foxes said goodnight and Marion went to her room shortly after.

By the time they were finishing their drinks in the third bar Val knew that trying to keep up with the youngsters had been a mistake. She thought that Carl and Libby drank too much but they were lightweights compared to this lot. She excused herself and told the others she was off back to the hotel. The youngsters said goodnight a little quickly, and Val's tipsy feeling left her as soon as the shock of the cold night air hit.

She didn't know this area of London particularly well and soon realized that she was lost.

'Damn!' she said out loud.

'You gotta problem?' answered a male voice, and Val felt the hairs stand up on the back of her neck. *Shit* she thought, but this time didn't say anything. She turned around slowly and looked at the three hooded youths. She was in trouble. The street wasn't well lit and they were the only ones on it. It was a pedestrian only area and Val looked around and knew that the chances of many people walking down this street were few and far between.

*****

Ron assumed that Claire was still resting. He hadn't seen her for a while and hadn't heard anything to the contrary from Gabriella. He'd watched the progress of Val's course on and off during the week and although he was pleased that she seemed a lot happier, was still against her going away to Africa. If he had his way Ron would have enveloped Val in a cocoon of cotton wool, making her safe and comfortable so that nothing would ever hurt her again. He knew that this was impractical and unrealistic but couldn't help himself. He'd checked on the kids from time to time and was happy with their progress. Although gutted that they'd lost their father they were young and healthy and had found it easier to cope and move on. Carl and Libby also had each other and a good support network of friends that they could rely on. Their mother was looking out for them but Ron noticed that she still seemed to be carrying around some guilt over his death and he couldn't understand why. This convinced him that she wasn't ready for the major challenge of working in a foreign country.

With these thoughts in mind Ron hovered just above the pavement and took in the scene of three youths taunting his wife and a fourth, watching and laughing. Ron felt his anger rising and he started shaking. One of the youths brandished a knife and Val

94

started to back off until another moved quickly behind her and the third to the side so that she had no escape route without making contact with one of them. Had Ron looked harder he would have noticed that the fourth youth appeared to be dressed as if from a different era, but he was too intent on the situation with his wife.

'Hand over your bag and I might not hurt you.'

Val's eyes moved from side to side, looking at the youths and trying to figure out an escape route. She knew she had no chance and was terrified. She also realized that she was absolutely furious. Sensing that the boys would attack whether or not she complied, Val carefully lifted her bag strap over her head. Her pulse was racing as if her heart would explode from her body at any second, and she acted as if she was going to hand the bag over. Val's world went into slow motion as she swung her bag back behind her and then forward, hitting the knifed youth on the arm that held the weapon, and knocking it out of his hand. It took a moment for the gang to react - they hadn't expected this from the scared looking middle-aged woman. Val took advantage and took off as if being chased by all hell's demons.

The fourth youth had watched the scene unfold and as Val ran off he threw a dustbin lid directly into her path. Ron was amazed that even in her panicked state, Val hadn't seen him do this. She tripped and fell heavily into the gutter and Ron summoned all his strength and approached the youth, hoping that he had the power to move or throw an object to frighten or even hurt him. He didn't expect to be seen and was taken aback when the youth turned and gave him a wicked smile, before running at him full pelt. The momentum of the impact threw Ron to the ground and he felt himself being punched and kicked as if he had a proper human form, and feeling pain from each strike.

The youth had the advantage of surprise and Ron's pathetic attempts to return the teenager's punches received derisive laughter and taunts. He tried his utmost to stand and push him away so he could see what was happening to Val, but became weaker with every blow. Although he struggled to the last Ron eventually passed out, the boy still taunting him until he could hear no more.

Val's thoughts came flooding in as she tried to make sense of what was happening. Even in her frightened and disturbed state she knew that the dustbin lid had flown through the air unaided, without the assistance of a gust of wind or anything else for that matter. Seeing the hooded youths walking purposely toward her, Val attempted to get up. She winced when she tried to put weight on her foot and knew that put paid to any further attempt at escape. She closed her eyes for a second, trying to prepare herself for the inevitable pain that was to follow.

Val tried her hardest not to shake and act cowardly. She didn't want the violent bullies to win even though she was terrified. Pressing her hands onto the pavement to support her, she slowly stood up and relieved the pressure on her ankle by standing fully on one leg, only the toes of the other foot contacting the pavement. Although her tormentors were amazed at the dustbin lid that had caused Val's fall, the only thing they cared about was that their victim hadn't escaped. The youth with the knife looked at her foot and then at his accomplices to ensure that they were watching. Sadistically and violently he kicked without warning and she screamed in agony and fell to the pavement again trying to relieve the pressure on her foot to alleviate the pain. All the time she had held onto her bag, but not for much longer. She felt the knife cut the strap and the blade contacted her waist and the side of her forearm that was trying to protect her possessions.

One of the other youths was given the bag and he emptied the contents out onto the street, taking her purse and mobile phone and leaving the other items scattered along the pavement.

'Get up!' said the knife holder and Val slowly pulled herself onto her feet, dreading what was coming.

'Take her coat first.' He nodded to one of his crew and the boy tugged her coat off her. All thoughts of being brave disappeared when Val realized what they had in mind and she shook her head repeatedly.

'No! Oh no! Just take what you have and leave me. Please.' She was hugging herself and shaking.

The hoodie with the knife handed his weapon over to one of his accomplices as he undid his belt and started unzipping his jeans. He nodded to the third hoodie who grabbed Val's arms and put them behind her back. She was frantic now and started to scream, trying to wriggle out of the thug's grip. They stopped for a second as they heard footsteps and a couple appeared from around the corner, the woman linking arms with the man and laughing up into his face. They stopped laughing as soon as they saw the scene ahead of them and the man quickly took out his mobile, dialled a number and talked into the phone.

The two accomplices looked at their leader for advice.

'Go,' he said as he quickly secured his jeans and belt. He gave Val a swift and painful kick to the shin and ran off, but not before the quick thinking woman had taken a photograph on her mobile phone. The couple ran to Val's side and gently supported her as she collapsed to the floor, shaken and terrified from her ordeal.

The police and an ambulance arrived and Val was taken to the hospital to be checked over. Her waist was grazed but the cut on her arm had to be stitched and Val's ankle wasn't broken, but badly sprained. Her face was grazed from the fall onto the pavement and the gutter, and her hands were cut and tiny stones had to be removed from the cuts by a nurse with a tweezers. While she was being checked over and patched up Val had asked the police to contact Marion to let her know what had happened. They also helped her contact her credit card and mobile phone providers and a stop was put on both. She cancelled her other cards by contacting her bank and she was so glad that she'd left her house keys in the hotel, even though they didn't identify her address. She was able to concentrate while doing this and it wasn't until she'd given a statement and the police were taking her back to the hotel that delayed shock started to set in. Despite her injuries Val knew that it could have been worse and she would be forever grateful to the people who stopped the attack from going any further. Regardless, she was still frightened and upset and just wanted to go home.

By the time Val arrived at the hotel Marion was beside herself with worry. She had no idea how she would feel under the same circumstances, but knew that she'd want the comfort of familiar things and the security of her own home. Marion had therefore packed her own belongings and as much of Val's as she could. A policewoman brought Val up to the hotel room and she fell into Marion's hug, grateful for the security of her friend. The embrace shocked Marion but she held Val and comforted her through her painful sobs. When the sobs abated she sat her down on the bed, the policewoman sitting patiently at the desk all the while.

'What have they done to you?' Marion looked at the dishevelled Val and stroked her cheek. The policewoman looked at both women and read something into their relationship that wasn't there, being unaware of the circumstances that had cemented their friendship. She coughed and both women turned to her, their former intimacy broken.

'I want to go home,' said Val and Marion nodded and told her that most of her things had been packed.

'We don't usually do this but I'll ask my Sarge if we can take you. It's only right after what you've been through.'

Marion smiled at the policewoman, grateful for her compassion. She checked them out while the officer sat in reception with Val and it wasn't long before they were making their way to Val's home in the police car. The two constables came in with them and told Val that they'd be back the following morning to go through her statement again and to inform her of any progress. Marion closed the door and made her way to the kitchen to make them both a hot sweet drink. She had a feeling that the attack had put paid to Val's working trip to Zambia. If this was the case Marion would also postpone her own trip and make her number one priority to look after her friend, and get her back on her feet after her terrifying ordeal.

*****

Ron tried to open his eyes but they felt as if they were stuck together. He struggled and eventually they opened. They felt swollen and when he touched his nose, he knew that something wasn't right. There weren't any mirrors so he couldn't look at his face but by the way he felt, knew that he had at least one black eye and possibly a broken nose. He was aching and bruised but these pains were minor compared to his feelings of inadequacy at not being able to help his wife. He was so relieved that the two people had arrived in the nick of time and Val's attack hadn't been even worse. He called for Claire but there was no reply. To his surprise Gabriella appeared. Her eyes took in the

99

state of him and he felt as if he was being evaluated as well as examined.

'I see you've met one of the devil's servants.'

So that was it. It made sense to him now and he simply nodded.

'Tell me what happened.' Ron was surprised that Gabriella didn't already know and she explained that angels weren't able to follow the lives of every human being all of the time.

'We can't prevent all evil, Ron. But do what we can.'

Ron thought he'd never know how things worked in his new home and he wasn't too fussed about finding out at present. His top priority was his wife's wellbeing and that's what he told Gabriella, after explaining what had happened to Val. The angel remained silent, contemplating the events and action to be taken. Ron wanted action straight away and was unusually impatient.

'I'm going to get Claire,' he said. 'Claire, Claire, Claire!' She could hear her name being called over and over, but didn't want to respond. She was still extremely tired and not yet ready to return. She tried to ignore it but Ron's annoying voice refused to go away.

'What is it?' This was the closest Claire had felt to being hung over since her death.

'About time. What kept you?' He didn't wait for a response, 'We need to get back to Earth ASAP, we've got work to do.'

Claire took in Ron's sorry state and her curiosity made her forget about her tiredness.

'What's happened? Are you okay? Who did that to you?'

Gabriella listened as Ron explained and when she'd heard enough she interrupted. 'Why don't you both visit her and see how she's getting on. You may be surprised when you see what's been happening while you've been resting, Claire,' she added mysteriously, and Claire's interest was certainly piqued. When she'd established that Ron's injuries would heal quickly, she was eager to get on.

'Let's go, I haven't got all day to hang around this place.'

Gabriella hid a smile as they disappeared and before long, arrived at Val's house.

Chapter 8

Graham hadn't told his sons or his estranged wife his new address and refused to answer his phone. After their visit from Claire, Jim and Tony were extremely worried about their father. Even though she was dead they knew their sister wouldn't let it rest until they'd been to see him. Both were still angry with him but neither wished him ill. The time had come for action and they had coerced his boss into giving them his new address, using emotional blackmail as the lever.

'So,' said Tony, on the phone to Adrian Walker. 'We know our father is depressed and if he attempts to take his life and we've been unable to contact him because you've withheld his address...'

'All right. All right. Just wait a minute.' He buzzed his secretary and she'd looked up the details on the company database. 'If this goes wrong I'll deny any knowledge, so don't tell him you got his address from me.' Tony thanked him politely and hung up. And now they were outside the front door of their father's apartment block, both hesitant to knock.

'How do you start to explain how annoyed you are without tipping him over the edge?' asked Jim and his brother shrugged. They'd have to play it by ear and try not to lose their temper. The aim was to get their father well again. The recriminations could follow once he'd come through the current crisis.

The twins could hear the noise from the TV inside the flat so knew he must be in. He'd get fed up with the knocking before them so they carried on until they heard a shuffling noise from inside.

'Keep your hair on, I'm coming.'

The door opened a crack and Graham tried to push it closed as soon as he recognized his sons. He was too slow and Jim had a foot in the door and Tony opened it wider, accidentally banging it into his father.

'Ouch. For Christ's sake,' Graham stood there rubbing his arm without inviting his sons inside. They looked at their father trying to hide their shock. He'd always been big but muscular, not fat. Now that muscle had turned to fat and a big belly dangled out from underneath the stained sweatshirt that was too small for him. His tracksuit trousers were also stained in the groin and the legs. There was more grey in his greasy hair and, as he hadn't bothered shaving, there was an uneven growth on his face. Still no invitation so the twins walked into their father's home. Graham sank down onto the settee and Tony moved the empty crisp and biscuit packets and sat next to him, trying not to scratch at imagined bugs. Jim took the chair opposite.

'I suppose I should offer you a cup of tea or something?'

'I'll do it, Dad.' Tony went to the small kitchen, which was in an even worse state. He walked back into the living room in disgust.

'How the fuck have you let this happen?' His hands gestured to his father and then to the flat. 'If it was one of us in this state, you'd go mental.'

Without saying a word Graham lifted his head and looked at each son in turn. A tear escaped an eye and he didn't bother wiping it away. It was soon accompanied by another and another and it wasn't long before he was sobbing like a child. Nobody had seen Graham cry like this before and in perfectly synchronized movements, a son sat either side of him. Jim hugged his father until the sobs subsided. When Graham came up for air, Tony put a reassuring arm around him.

'I'm sorry, Dad. But what's happened to you?'

Graham took a deep breath and his whole body shuddered. He calmed himself down and tried to find the words to explain.

'Your sister. I could cope with everything else, but your sister.' He shook his head and took another few breaths, desperately fighting back more tears and needing his sons to know how he'd ended up in his current condition.

'Can you walk or are you physically ill?' asked Jim and Graham said that he could move, but didn't have the inclination or willpower to do anything.

'Right, this is what we're going to do. We're going to get you packed and you're coming to stay with us for a while.'

Graham started to shake his head in protest. The twins ignored him.

'We'll get someone in to sort the flat out so that it's clean and tidy when you come back,' said Tony and Graham knew he was beaten.

'At least someone still cares.'

'You can tell us all about your other little family and our half-sister later,' said Tony and Graham knew he had a difficult time ahead. He didn't have an excuse for what he'd done and wasn't sure whether it would be more difficult to explain about his other family, or to get back to his previous good health.

*****

Three weeks had passed since the mugging and the attack had aged Val. Not normally a nervy person, she was now anxious and jumpy and worried about everything. Marion had made a brief visit to Yorkshire to finalise the house sale and Libby had stayed with her mother until she'd returned to London. They all agreed that Marion and Val would be great company for each other and Val didn't know how she would have got through the post mugging weeks without the support and company of her new friend.

'Today's the day then,' said Val and Marion nodded. They were waiting for a call from the charity to tell them whether there would be a place for them both on the Zambia trip. Marion knew that even if they were offered a place, Val was in no fit state to go. She was happy to give up her place on this occasion and until Val was more like her old self.

'You know I can't go don't you?' Val was squeezing her hands. A habit she'd picked up since the attack.

'Of course you can't, it's far too soon.'

'You know I'll never be the same person don't you?'

'Val, time's a great healer and you will get through this, otherwise they've won.'

Val said nothing and the phone rang. She looked at Marion who answered and it was the call they'd been waiting for. Marion put it onto loudspeaker as they listened to the news that they'd been selected to go to Zambia. Marion declined on behalf of them both. Gail knew about the attack and understood.

'The next trip is in the summer. Would you like to be considered for that one?'

'Yes please for both of us,' Marion ignored Val's look, 'we've already discussed this.' After a few niceties they hung up with Gail promising that she would be in touch.

'Why did you lie to her?'

'Because the summer will give you something to aim for. I know what happened was horrendous, Val, but you have to move on with your life.'

'Maybe if they'd been caught I could. But knowing that they're still out there probably attacking other people makes it almost impossible.

Marion understood and thought she would feel the same. If only there was something that could be done to catch the swine, Val would be able to move on with her life a lot easier.

*****

'Val needs our help. We have to do something and, sooner rather than later.' Ron was drumming his fingers, impatience getting the better of him.

'Hmm.' Claire was preoccupied. So her mother had moved in with Val and seemed to have had a personality transplant. She considered her mother's performance, as that's what she thought it was. In a crisis Claire's father had always taken charge and she hadn't thought her mother had it in her to be so strong and supportive.

'I suppose you have to be strong if you have three kids. We probably just didn't notice when we were young.'

Ron didn't have a clue what Claire was talking about and told her so. She explained herself and he was exasperated.

'That's all very well, Claire and I'm so glad that you're impressed by your mother.' She missed the sarcasm. 'But, we need to come up with a plan to get the muggers caught so that my wife can get better.'

'But I thought you didn't want her to go and work for the charity?'

'I want her to be well and happy and if that means she spreads her wings, well so be it. And anyway, your mother and my wife will look after each other, I can sense it,' he winked at Claire. 'So down to the business in hand. Catching the muggers.'

Claire listened intently while Ron explained his plan.

'So, let me get this right. Because we can't catch them ourselves, you want me to contact my brothers and ask Jim to use his girlfriend as bait so that they can catch the muggers?'

'In a nutshell, yes,' said Ron.

'Have you totally lost it?'

'Look. We have to do a bit first and track them down. You don't need to contact the twins before then.'

Even though Claire couldn't believe what she was hearing, she knew that she'd go along with Ron's plan and help him as much as she could. She hated the fact that the people who'd attacked Val were still at large and that other women could also be in danger.

'They're bloody cowards, Ron and I'll help if I can.' Seeing his smile was all the response that Claire needed. 'But before we go looking for the baddies, can we go and visit my father to see how he's getting on?'

Although impatient to find the muggers, Ron knew that he wouldn't have Claire's full attention until she'd seen her father. Having no choice, he agreed reluctantly and they soon found themselves in the twins' apartment.

The three men were in the lounge having just finished their Chinese takeaway. Claire was pleased to see that her father was in clean clothes and that some colour had returned to his cheeks. He was still overweight but looked as if he'd lost a little and he didn't have that desperate look about him.

Graham still hadn't explained how his second family had come about. He was on the mend and the twins judged that the time was right. Jim nodded to his brother without his father seeing.

'So what's our sister like then, Dad?' asked Tony, and Graham smiled.

'Fifteen and impulsive.'

'Like Claire,' said the boys and Graham laughed at their response.

'Very much so. She looks like Claire too, but taller and her hair's light and straight,' he paused for a second, considering. 'They share the same sense of humour, although Mel can be more serious.'

Claire was curious and looking forward to seeing Mel. The twins liked the picture their father was painting and were anxious to meet her.

'I don't know when I'll be able to arrange that.' Graham explained that Mel had been furious when he'd told her about them and had refused to speak to him since.

'Understandable I suppose.'

'So they didn't know about us either?' asked Jim.

'Carol did. But we never got around to telling Mel. Then after Claire went.' He took a moment to compose himself again, finding it difficult with every mention of his late daughter's name.

'I was sick of living a lie and your sister's passing made me realize what a bastard I'd been to everyone.' He waited for his sons to disagree but they said nothing.

'The day your mother threw me out was the day I was going to come clean and explain everything to her.'

The twins looked sceptical.

'Honestly, it's the truth. But I can understand why you wouldn't believe it after everything else that's happened. You can imagine how amazed I was when I discovered that your mother had known about Carol and Mel for some time.'

Their mother had been evasive when explaining the situation to them and the twins had suspected she knew more than she'd let on. They nodded, encouraging their father to continue.

'Mel's furious with both of us and even refuses to see her mother at weekends. Carol's spoken to the mother of one of Mel's friends and allowed her to stay there.'

The twins looked confused so Graham added. 'She's at boarding school you see.'

It made sense now. 'So she's at school during the week and stays with a friend at weekends. She must feel as if nobody wants her,' said Tony.

Graham protested, 'It's not like that, son. She knows that I adore her but I'm trying to do what she wants and to give her some space.'

They weren't convinced. They remembered what Claire had been like as a teenager - stroppy and pretending to be confident to hide all of the real insecurities that she'd felt. Both thought that what their half-sister needed was to know that her parents loved her.

'Can you give us the school details so we can arrange to meet her?' Jim took out his phone ready to Google the details.

'Um, that's not such a good idea.'

'Why?'

'Because Carol told me that Mel is to have nothing to do with any of us. That includes me, you two, and your mother.'

'But, Dad,' Jim was trying to contain his anger. 'She's our half-sister whether Carol likes it or not and she may want to meet us. Surely it has to be Mel's choice?'

Their father refused to budge and the twins didn't want to push him, for fear of a lapse into his former state of depression.

'Beer anyone?' Tony passed them each a bottle and they settled down to watch the match. The discussion about their half-sister was over for the moment but Tony was already figuring out how he could interrogate a number of computer programmes and people he knew to get the details they needed about their sister. They would find her and visit her. Their mother wouldn't be happy but they knew she was preoccupied looking after her new friend, so didn't plan on telling her for now.

Graham had a feeling that his sons would use their own means to find Mel and he was secretly glad. He knew that he was being cowardly but had kept to his part of the bargain as far as Carol was concerned, so at least his conscience was clear on that small detail.

*****

Claire considered what she'd heard but wasn't entirely satisfied.

'Why didn't they ask him why he wanted an affair in the first place and what made him and Carol decide to have a child? What went wrong with my parents' marriage? Why didn't they ask him that? Didn't he think my mother would find out? Why didn't he just tell her and ask for a divorce? What about both of them deceiving us, only his is the worst? Why...?'

'Enough!' shouted Ron. 'I don't know why they didn't ask those questions. Perhaps your father wouldn't have answered them or perhaps they think what's done is done and it doesn't matter now...'

'But of course it matters. I have a sister that I'm never going to meet. And their marriage has been a lie for at least fifteen years and they should have told us.' She angrily wiped away a tear and folded her arms. 'So much of my life was a lie Ron and they should have bloody well told us.'

'I'm sorry, Claire,' He took one of her hands and held it. 'I can understand you being annoyed, but you can't change the past. People have to live their own lives and make their own mistakes, Claire and, hopefully, learn from them.'

'I know you're right but it doesn't make it any easier to bear. I seem to have been constantly angry since we've been here, Ron and I wonder if any of the people I loved when I was alive were totally honest with me.'

'Your mother was trying to protect you, Claire. I know that because I'm a parent and that's what we do, so don't be angry with her. Although it takes two to make a marriage, your mother didn't deserve to be treated the way your father treated her, and she doesn't deserve your anger now.'

Claire knew that made sense. 'And my brothers always looked out for me. I so hope I don't find out that they're gangsters or spies or something.'

Ron laughed and Claire gave him a look. 'I'm serious you know.'

'Stop being such a drama queen and let's go and find these muggers.'

They were both surprised that instead of arriving on Earth they found themselves on the cream sofa, Gabriella sitting waiting for them with a folder in her hands.

'I have something to show you,' she said looking down and Claire and Ron followed her direction.

*****

Ken was breathing again but knew straight away that he wasn't in a human body. He tried to take a breath but even that felt strange. Suddenly, he was able to look around him and discovered that he was in a water world packed tightly with silvery fish. One or two near him changed direction and Ken felt himself move with them. Okay, so he was part of the shoal. As the shoal moved one way then another Ken saw a number of large shadows. He kept moving with the other fish and noticed it was getting brighter above the water. He wondered what was happening and felt

111

himself being pushed tightly into the fish nearest him. He didn't have to swim, the momentum of the others took him forward and gave him time to have a proper look around. He saw a number of dolphins moving back and forth and the realization dawned that his shoal was being herded into shallow waters. He knew how clever dolphins were and hoped that they'd recognize him as a former human and not eat him. He didn't have time to think further as they were now in shallow water and a few dolphins had started beating their tails on the silty seabed. A ring of mud appeared and he was startled by the panicked fish around him who were jumping into the air to avoid the mud ring. Unable to help himself his body took off, and the last thing he saw was the open-mouthed dolphin smiling happily at him. Ken tried shouting that it was a mistake and that he used to be human. The pretty mammal took no notice and halved his body before swallowing it in a few gulps.

The scene below Ron and Claire disappeared and they looked at Gabriella waiting for the explanation.

'See what happens when you're a bad person.'

'But he's not a thief or murderer, Gabriella. He was a good mate to me and looked after me by giving me a job.'

'You weren't the only one he was looking after.'

Ron was confused at Gabriella's enigmatic response and Claire thought there must be more to this that they weren't aware of. Not being one to keep her opinions to herself, she voiced her concern.

'He must have done something terrible that you don't know about, Ron. What has he done?'

'Very perceptive, Claire. What I need to know is whether you think his evil should be forgiven?'

'Why are you asking me, Gabriella? He hasn't done anything to me?'

Ron shook his head. 'Nor me.'

'You're both wrong. Claire. Let me show you something first.'

They watched as the scene below them unfolded. Two girls of indeterminate teenage age were in a taxi with a large man. They didn't recognize any of them. They were all laughing and joking and discussing the party they were about to attend. The man was promising lots of fun, free booze, food, dancing and anything else they might want. The girls were excited about sneaking out when they should have been in the school, doing their homework. Claire watched with a feeling of unease and her intuition served her well as they saw the car leave the party later on. The girls seemed unnaturally quiet and Claire noticed their faces were very pale and they looked shocked and sad. The big man was still smiling and laughing and the girls appeared upset to Claire, one of them leaning against the side of the car, trying to be as far away from the big man as she could get. When he smiled and told them to cheer up, the other returned his smile, but it was forced and didn't reach her eyes.

'What's he done to them and what's this got to do with me, and Ron's boss Ken?'

'The large man in the car is known to the criminal fraternity as Big Ed. He uses his considerable charm to groom girls and when they trust him, takes advantage of their naivety to convince them they'll have a wonderful time at his parties.'

'Oh my God,' said Ron, 'he's using them as teenage prostitutes?'

Gabriella's eyes answered the question and Claire's hands flew to her mouth in horror.

'These girls think they're going to a free party and instead they're getting raped?'

'Yes, in a nutshell - but it's not that simple, Claire. Their drinks are spiked and by the time they come round they only know what's happened by the way they feel. Some of them he uses once – his so called clients like young, fresh girls – the girls who are dependent on drugs are used on a regular basis and he provides them with their *hit* in return. It doesn't take long for them to feel worthless and he collects them every week and puts them through the same hell. Even the girls who are only used once are threatened with consequences if they tell anyone what's happened. Inevitably, they're too scared to tell anyone.'

'I still don't understand...'

'Ken worked for Big Ed. Your newly discovered sister was involved but had a bad feeling about the night they were being taken to their first party. She had the presence of mind to insist that the taxi was stopped and she got out. She only tried drugs once by the way and that was enough for her.'

'So Mel and these girls...' Gabriella put her hand up to silence Claire.

'These girls, Claire are nothing to do with your sister. He has already used her best friends, but won't be using them again because they're too damaged by the experience and of no further use to him.'

For once Claire was lost for words. Ron wasn't and he banged a fist on the sofa arm in fury.

'So the bastard who I thought was my best mate was knowingly taking young girls to be deflowered! No, raped, and being paid to do so?'

Gabriella nodded sadly.

'And you want to know whether we should forgive him?' asked Claire.

Gabriella nodded again. 'He's shown some remorse and the Committee will decide whether he should be given another chance. They want the opinion of some of the people whose lives he's affected.'

'I say let the bastard suffer...'

'There's more, Ron.'

114

'I don't need to see anything else, my mind's made up. He deserves all he gets.'

Claire agreed and inclined her head to show her solidarity with Ron.

Gabriella looked directly at Ron.

'Are you certain you don't wish to know what else your friend was up to?'

Ron didn't have the stomach to view any more footage of the man he thought he knew and Gabriella decided the biggest shock could wait.

'So be it,' she said. 'Time to go.'

'But what about those poor girls? What's going to happen to them?'

'Their physical suffering will soon be over.' She disappeared into the ether and both Claire and Ron hoped she meant their persecutor would be caught. The alternative was too dreadful to imagine.

Chapter 9

After witnessing the dilemma of the poor young girls, Ron and Claire were even more determined to catch the thugs who had mugged Val. They felt as if they were on a quest to avenge all victims of crime and it was with this attitude that they arrived in the area where Val had been attacked. Two weeks of constant vigilance followed with zero results. They'd witnessed a few drunken brawls, an argument over a parking space that had turned violent, and an amorous couple who'd been arrested for performing an indecent act in public. Their patience was waning when they reluctantly decided that this would be the final weekend before taking a break from this part of London to see how their respective families and friends were getting on. Claire stopped daydreaming as she saw three hooded youths turn the corner onto the street. One leant against a wall and lit a cigarette and one of the others followed suit. The first took a knife out of his pocket and started pushing it into the concrete on the wall between the gaps. Claire nudged Ron but he'd already seen them and from the look on his face she knew that this was the gang that had attacked Val.

They watched for a while. A few men had passed the youths and the three hadn't reacted. Claire rightly assumed that they were cowards, as bullies usually were. Two women walked down the street and the leader of the three nodded to his companions. A crowd of men appeared behind them all wearing t-shirts that bore comments about a certain Gary, a stag party Claire assumed, and the women passed without bother from the youths. Claire contemplated fate as the women would never know what the immediate future could have held for them had the stag party decided to go in a different direction. Ron brought her back to the present when the youths moved away from the street. The spirits followed.

By the end of that evening Ron and Claire were extremely pleased with themselves. Their patience had paid off and they had memorized the addresses of the three. Within a few days they knew their names, their habits, what they liked to eat and drink and some knowledge of their family members. Claire laughed sadly when Ron told her that the gang leader Mikey, was scared of rats and that his mother woke him up by taking him a cup of tea every morning.

'How can he be so boyish at home and so cruel when he's out with his friends?' Neither had the answer and just wanted them all to be brought to justice quickly so that Val could move on with her life.

*****

Jim and Tony thought it would be easy to find their new sister without their father's assistance but they were wrong. It hadn't occurred to them that she would have a different surname and Graham had refused to share. They had checked all boarding schools in a 300-mile radius via Internet search engines. There were too many to visit and even if they decided to go to each one, the twins would have been uncomfortable having to explain the reason for visiting. They also knew their sister would probably not agree to see them even if they managed to find her this way. They were contemplating their dilemma when Claire and Ron decided to pay them a visit.

'Do you think I should visit their dreams again?' Claire asked Ron and Tony looked at his brother.

'Don't ask me how I know but Claire wants to talk to us.'

'I know.'

Ron noticed Claire's surprise when he saw that her mouth was hanging open and her eyes were enlarged like a bush baby's trying to see in its dark surroundings.

'Tell them you want them to capture Val's muggers.' He whispered even though the twins couldn't hear him.

'What?'

'I don't know how it works but it appears your brothers know you want to talk. Quickly! Concentrate and tell them.'

'Who's Val?' asked Jim, 'Ah.' He understood as the thoughts from Claire floated into his mind.

'You want us to capture her muggers, Claire? Is that right?' Claire smiled and nodded and Ron gritted his teeth in frustration.

'It's no good nodding and smiling like an idiot. They can't see you.'

'Claire, are you still there? Claire?' Her mind had wandered and the messages to her brothers were becoming disjointed.

'Dad's getting better, and yes we'll make sure he loses more weight.'

'No we don't know why he did it.'

The brothers were playing conversation tag. Fascinating as it was to watch, Ron needed Claire to focus on the main reason for their visit. He elbowed her to get her full attention.

'Can we concentrate on the muggers for a moment, please?' She looked like a startled rabbit but was listening. 'Tell them we know where they live and we want them to catch them in the act and hand them into the police.'

Claire obliged and her brothers were stunned.

'But how are we supposed to do that?'

'Jim's girlfriend,' said Ron, and Claire was as astonished as her brothers when she relayed the message to them.

'Even she seemed surprised by that request,' said Tony. 'Which makes me think she's not acting on her own here.'

'Claire, who's with you? Where do these guys live? Claire, Claire?'

Other questions followed but these were the last ones she heard. The absolute concentration had worn Claire out and she couldn't stay with it. Ron's voice was cajoling and she fought the exhaustion for a few more seconds before the darkness and bliss of absolute peace took hold.

The twins eventually stopped talking to Claire, finally realizing that she was no longer with them.

'Did that really happen?' they asked each other, flabbergasted by their encounter with their sister but overjoyed that she was back in their lives.

'Okay, so she's dead but can still speak to us. Does that make us mediums or something?' Jim had wondered the same and said as much. 'I'm just happy that it isn't the end and that she seems to be okay.' Although this wasn't their first contact with Claire they still found it unnerving. Both were pale and Jim was shaking from the experience. They sat in silence for a few minutes contemplating the consequences of regular contact with their dead sister.

When he'd calmed down enough to stop shaking, Jim broke the silence, 'Do you think we should ask Dad more questions?'

Tony shook his head. 'I don't know what to think,' he tapped his fingers together in agitation. 'Actually, I do. I think we shouldn't tell anyone about

119

our conversations with Claire just yet. They'll think we're mad.'

It was a lot to take in and they would have thought anyone who explained the same experience as totally bonkers.

'But we need to tell Fiona about the plan,' said Jim, and his brother raised his eyebrows.

'Are you serious? Do you really plan on using Fiona as bait to catch these muggers?'

Jim didn't have a chance to respond as Tony continued, 'For one thing it would be far too dangerous and for another, we don't even know where they hang out.'

'We could ask the woman they mugged.'

Tony shook his head. 'And how do we explain the rest?'

'Fair point. We won't do anything just yet but I'm sure it's not the last we'll hear of this.'

That was the only part of the conversation the twins agreed on. Knowing their sister as they did, they knew it wouldn't be too long before they heard from her again. And the knowledge that she was in regular contact with them even under the current circumstances was a huge comfort to both men.

*****

Nobody was about when Claire woke up after visiting her brothers so she decided to visit her mother.

It was night time and Val had already gone to bed. They'd had a lovely evening. Marion had cooked one of her delicious stews and they'd had a few glasses of wine later on while watching a soppy movie. They'd both cried, ostensibly because of the film but Marion knew that they were really crying for other reasons. Neither needed to explain. Their feelings were in perfect sync and they drew great comfort from each other. Marion took the glasses to the kitchen deciding

120

not to wash-up until morning. Before her life had disintegrated she had been manically obsessed about all aspects of housework and tidiness and nothing was allowed to be out of place. As she walked up the stairs, Claire realized that her mother's change in habits and personality were a revelation to her.

Marion used the bathroom, removed her make-up and cleaned her teeth. She turned on the bedside lamp, turned off the main light and got into bed. She cleared her throat and Claire wondered why her mother was acting as if she was about to give a speech. She didn't have to ponder for very long.

'Hi, Claire,' said Marion. 'Well, today's been a pretty uneventful day. The man in the shop on the corner tried to sell me potatoes that were almost sprouting. I soon put him in his place. We're all well down here but I can't say it's getting any easier. Your bastard father is still sponging off your brothers as far as I'm aware and your brothers have been behaving quite strangely just lately. I don't mean their normal weird twin behaviour. By the way I've done a bit of research about that and it's common amongst twins but almost unheard of for a non-twin sibling to be involved in their telepathy. What do you think of that then? Anyway as I was saying. They sorted your room at the house without being asked. I was happy to let them do it but got the feeling that they were up to something. We shall see.'

'Now that I don't have you all to worry about I've decided to concentrate on Val and help her to get her life back on track. It'll be easier when they catch the scum who attacked her and I hope the police get their act together and do that quickly, Claire. You know we're not going away with the charity this time but I'm hoping she's going to be in the right frame of mind to go in the summer.' Marion stopped talking and looked around the room. Telling her daughter all about the day's events and her innermost thoughts had made her feel a lot closer to her. Tonight however, Marion sensed a presence and felt a connection that she hadn't felt since the day her daughter died.

'You're here aren't you? I know, Claire.'

'Yes, Mum I am. I can hear you,' Claire shouted in excitement, thinking that her mother might be able to see her. 'Over here,' she called and waved.

It was the first time since her daughter's death that Marion was convinced that she could actually sense her presence. She looked around the room but Claire knew that her mother couldn't see her and she concentrated hard and doubled her efforts.

'I'm fine, Mum. Please don't worry about me. I'm watching over all of you.'

In Marion's thoughts her daughter's voice was as clear as day. She gasped as she sat bolt upright in her bed and looked around the room. She didn't see anything but still sensed Claire's presence. Tears were streaming uncontrollably down her face as she tried to breathe properly so she could speak.

'I love you my darling daughter. I always have and I always will.' The sobbing was now under control and Marion smiled at various spots around the room hoping that her daughter could see her. 'Tonight you've given me the strength I need to get on with my life and I'm going to make you proud. It's such a comfort knowing that you're watching out for us. I miss you so much, Claire.'

'I miss you too, Mum.' Her mother didn't acknowledge this last message and Claire concentrated and doubled her efforts trying to get the message to her mother.

As quickly as she'd sensed her daughter's presence it disappeared and Marion knew she'd gone. She lay back on the bed. Although Claire's message was a massive comfort it also heightened her loss and the tears came, as they had done every night since her daughter's passing.

Claire was crying too. Her family weren't particularly demonstrative and she could count on one hand the number of times her mother had said she loved her. In their home, love had been shown in deeds rather than words and although she knew she was loved, it was very rarely talked about. She was so grateful for that small contact and knew that her mother would take comfort from it, even though she'd been sobbing her heart out when she'd left her. Claire laughed when she realized that her mother had talked to her every night and vowed to visit more so that she could catch up on all of her news. Having left her mother Claire wanted to go and visit Jay. She knew that he was now well but had an overwhelming urge to be close to him.

After resting awhile, she was pleased to see that Jay was putting his life back together and had started work as an assistant chef in the hotel managed by his uncle. It was a large concern and there were plenty of staff. The kitchen staff and waiters were finishing up the nightshift and Claire had witnessed a few of the females flirting with Jay. She felt jealous. Although she'd been the love of his life and wanted him to move on, actually seeing him laugh and joke with other girls unsettled her. Claire was in this frame of mind when Ron and Gabriella found her. They sensed straight away that something was wrong and she told them about both her visits and explained the reasons for her melancholy. They were pleased to hear the news about her mother and Gabriella told her it was common for bereaved parents to talk to their dead children.

'It can be such a comfort to both parents and children, but you have to accept that your contact with your mother was a one-off.' Claire knew there was no point in asking why and Gabriella smiled, pleased with

123

Claire's progress. 'As for Jay, he will always love you, Claire, and you will always love him. But you have to let him go now and give him permission to carry on with his life.'

'He doesn't need my permission.' Claire knew that she sounded like a truculent child, but felt unable to help herself.

Gabriella glided to her side and took her in her arms. A surge of warmth and energy passed through her, and her uncertainty disappeared. When Gabriella let her go, Claire felt as if she had reached a new level of understanding and genuinely wanted Jay to move forward with his life.

'Something's changed and I feel more grown up and tolerant.'

Gabriella and Ron smiled at her and Claire resisted the urge to put her hands together in the prayer position and bow to them both. She hadn't totally grown up then!

Gabriella left shortly after and Ron and Claire decided it was time for more detective work. They knew her brothers would take some convincing to trap the muggers but if their plan worked, they would be able to dangle a carrot that the twins would be unable to resist.

*****

Drew's screaming woke Mel. She must be having another nightmare, thought Mel. Her friend hadn't been the same since the night she'd gone with Big Ed in the taxi and Mel knew that something sinister had taken place. She also knew that Drew was frightened and she would have to take it easy with her. She got out of bed and walked over to her bed. Drew's body was thrashing from side to side but she'd stopped screaming. She was moaning now and saying the word no, over and over again. Mel sat on the bed and took hold of the hand with which she was hitting herself.

'Wake up, Drew. It's okay. Wake up.'

She opened her eyes. Looking from side to side she immediately sat up. Forgetting where she was for a moment she grabbed her hand back from Mel and hugged herself. All Mel could see was the terror in her friend's eyes and knew that whatever was going on had to stop.

'Talk to me, Drew. Please.'

'I can't. You don't know what it's like.' She looked around the room, checking if anyone else was awake. 'If I tell, awful things could happen to me and Alice, or our families.'

'Is that what Big Ed said to you?'

'Never mind what he said Mel. You don't want to get involved, trust me.' She shuddered. 'Getting out of the taxi that night was the best thing you could have done.'

'Tell me what they did to you, Drew, please.'

'I can't, Mel. I'm sorry but I just can't.' She lay down with her back to Mel and tucked her knees up into her body, trying to make herself as small as possible.

'I'll have to help you if you can't help yourself,' whispered Mel to her friend's back.

*****

Since moving Jay's tablet bottle to stop him overdosing Claire and Ron hadn't been able to move any other objects, no matter how hard they'd tried. They'd witnessed a few other incidents after seeing the man throw himself under the train on the underground, but had been incapable of offering any physical assistance. Being unable to search through physical detail they pondered how they were going to discover details about Mel's school to pass to the twins.

'We may not be able to move stuff,' said Ron, 'but that doesn't stop us from looking.' Logical, thought

Claire and she agreed to his suggestion that they should start at her father's empty flat.

As promised by the twins the flat had been professionally cleaned and everything was sparkling and smelled fresh.

'Ooh, that's lovely,' said Claire and they remained still for a moment, taking in the smell of lavender polish in the living room and citrus in the kitchen.

'How come we can smell this?'

Here we go again thought Ron as he wondered why he was always expected to know the answers.

'No idea, but look.' He pointed to the coffee table where the fastidious cleaner had laid out all of Graham's mail. There were three separate piles. One for junk, one that looked like personal correspondence. 'Birthday cards,' said Claire. And the final pile looked like bill or invoice envelopes.

'And we've struck lucky.' Claire followed the direction of Ron's pointing finger to a white envelope with a postage stamp franked on the right-hand side. On the left hand corner of the envelope was a blue crest with the name *Manor Lodge Boarding School for Girls* and an address underneath. Ron lifted his hand and they high-fived each other.

'Clever man.'

'I'm not just a pretty face you know.' He fired a pretend punch in her direction when she screwed up her face at his comment.

'Shall we go visit?' Ron nodded and they were off to their new location.

The following morning was spent moving from classroom to classroom to try and identify Claire's half-sister. It was Ron who eventually found her in the dining room at lunchtime. She was at a table with two girls, heads bent in what looked to be a serious

126

conversation. Her hair was dark blonde and straight but the way she flicked it back was exactly the same as Claire did. He also noticed that she gave the same scathing look if she wasn't happy or didn't agree with what was being said. They zoomed in to listen and Ron felt like he was watching a younger version of his dead friend.

'...But I said to Drew last night that you can't go on like this,' Mel was addressing Alice. 'I know you won't talk about what happened but I'm not completely stupid you know.'

'We know you're not *completely* stupid.' Alice rolled her eyes in the way that only teenagers could. 'But you are completely naive if you think we can just grass up Big Ed without any consequences. We're lucky he doesn't want to use us any more so get over it.'

'But what if...'

Alice ignored her remark. 'When I told him I was going to report him; do you know what he said?' She had raised her voice and students at the other tables were starting to stare.

'Keep it down,' said Drew and Alice composed herself before continuing in a whisper. She leant forward.

'He said he would come for me and break my legs. Then he'd go after my family. He told me he knew stuff about my little brother, the school he goes to, his after school activities and how easy it would be for him to have...' She stumbled over the words and had to gather her wits again, biting her bottom lip before continuing. 'Big Ed said he could arrange an accident and that it would all be my fault.'

'But...'

'No buts, Mel. We can't do anything about it and like I said, he's leaving us alone now.' She smiled showing a confidence and false bravado that she didn't feel.

127

'And what about when he decides to pick on other, maybe younger girls who'll go through the same as you. Is that what you want?'

Alice pushed her chair away from the table and stood up, leaving her lunch untouched. 'Come on, Drew.'

'I can't save the whole world Mel! I'm damned if I do and damned if I don't.' Alice walked away shoulders hunched like a condemned man walking to the gallows.

Claire and Ron thought she sounded spent and beaten and a lot older than her fifteen or sixteen years. Mel was going to need the support of her brothers whether she asked for it or not and Claire planned to visit them as soon as possible.

Chapter 10

Ken was back on Earth and stood with his eyes closed, wondering what lay in store for him this time. He was terrified again and the worse thing was that nobody cared or would do anything to make him feel better. Before opening his eyes, he contemplated his human life and realized that he had been a weak and wicked man and now regretted the way he'd treated people. He should have kept in contact with his mother after she'd married her Asian boyfriend but couldn't help disliking him. It wasn't his fault that he disliked all foreigners. If only he'd tried to like them and the women he'd bedded, he might not be in his current predicament. Not only those that he'd loved, or should have loved, he corrected himself, but the girls in the taxi, some of whose lives he'd helped to put on the road to ruin. He should have refused Big Ed and told the authorities but had been too cowardly and greedy.

He had to stop thinking about his previous life and deal with the immediate situation. He sniffed and there was an overpowering smell of animals and manure. There was also a lot of bird and insect noise and it was unbearably hot. Here we go, thought Ken. He opened his eyes and took in the scene around him. He was amongst rolling grassland which was dotted with trees. The air was really dry and he was thirsty and hungry. He looked down at his striped body and realized that this time he'd returned as a zebra. The other zebras around him were grazing and he joined a small group and started eating. It wasn't the best food he'd ever tasted but he was happy that he'd progressed to mammal. In his tormented little mind, he wondered if this meant that eventually he'd be human again and his pain and suffering would be over.

The need to quench his thirst prevented any further thoughts and he wondered where their watering hole was. As he looked at the other animals in his group Ken saw their eyes darting around and their heads moving. They were getting skittish and the reason soon became apparent. The pride of lions had closed in stealthily and quietly and were a little way away, but heading in the direction of his group. He looked at the twenty or so other animals that he was with. Ken tried to work out whether he would be able to run faster than any, no, than one of them. I only have to outrun one, he thought, and I'll be able to escape. Then the penny dropped and the truth hit him like a hammer in the face. So this time his fate was to be ripped to pieces and eaten by the king of the jungle. Ken wasn't prepared to accept the inevitable without a fight. He moved toward the centre of the group and along with the other animals, started walking in the opposite direction of the lions. Their efforts were futile as the lions had them surrounded. The zebras started trotting and this soon turned into a full pelt gallop. Ken was out of breath and struggling to keep up but kept running out of sheer terror, and because his very life depended on it.

Using their instinct, the lions targeted him even before he fell behind the small herd. He felt one of the females closing in and he doubled his efforts even though he knew he'd had it. As she leapt onto his back, he hoped that his third animal death would be less painful than the other two. He'd seen images of lions killing their prey on television and assumed that his murderer would bite his neck, thereby severing his spinal cord, making him bleed to death by puncturing the jugular vein or even asphyxiating him. None of these methods were particularly appealing, but Ken was in for his last surprise of that day and his hopes were in vain. These weren't ordinary lions. One immobilized him by thrusting its teeth into his neck and another took a bite out of his stomach. He was able to see his entrails hanging out and could do absolutely nothing about it. The male came along and roared, the powerful noise blocking out Ken's screams. The excruciating pain and sound of being eaten alive by lions was his final memory as a zebra.

Ron and Claire had watched in horror and Gabriella had been looking at their reactions, and not at the demise of Ken.

'That's terrible.' Claire's face was pulled into a grimace. She'd wanted to look away but felt her eyes being drawn to the scene as if it were a horror movie. Only this time she didn't have a cushion to hide behind. She'd contemplated hiding behind the sofa until the macabre scene disappeared but had decided against it, believing the others would think her silly. Ron was also grimacing and shaking his head at the same time.

'Make it stop, Gabriella,' he pleaded.

Gabriella knew the suffering of souls like Ken was painful for kind, loving souls to watch. She couldn't intervene while at their current location so swept her arms above the scene to make it disappear.

'I have something very important to ask you both,' she turned to face them. 'Can you forgive him his wicked ways or do you think he deserves more of the same?'

Neither of them would wish that sort of suffering on their mortal enemies and that's what they told her.

'Right. I'm going to save his soul. These tasks are never easy and it's important that you stay here,' she looked at them each in turn, 'very important. Disturbance will be caused and sometimes souls can get mixed up in it, and end up going to the wrong place. Do you understand?'

After witnessing Ken's treatment at the hand of his masters in hell neither of them had any intention of risking that fate. They nodded vigorously and Gabriella deployed her wings and gently flapped each one in turn, as if testing.

'Until we meet again,' she said, and instead of the usual whoosh followed by her disappearance, she flapped her wings and hovered in the air before flying off at what Claire deemed to be warp factor ten.

On her journey Gabriella dodged the souls that were on their way up to Cherussola, her immediate concern for the one she wanted to save. The Committee gave dispensation to a number of the more experienced angels and if they thought that someone deserved another chance they were willing to review the case.

She arrived at her destination shortly after, warmed up and ready to face the action. She looked around and saw Ken's soul heading in the direction of one of the devil's servants. From Ron's description she recognized the youth who had attacked him when his wife was being mugged. Gabriella was affronted and tried to contain her fury, knowing that she would need her wits about her even to defeat this maggot. She was a grade 5 angel and from her estimation they'd sent a grade 1 or 2 demon. Ken's soul got closer and closer and the demon noticed that he was in competition for this one. He kicked and punched and she avoided both and ignored his taunts. The demon youth hesitated for a moment, unsure whether to concentrate on catching the soul or to attack the angel. He'd had similar animal experiences to Ken and didn't want to fail his masters by making the wrong decision. Gabriella took away his choice. A millisecond before Ken reached their location she gave a strong jab that the youth hadn't expected.

The momentum of the hit took him a distance away and she grabbed the soul of Ken.

She knew it wouldn't be long before others pursued her and she took off in the frame of mind that all hell's servants were following. Had the youth done his job properly, this would have been a canny estimation of the truth. Unfortunately for him, he hadn't had the presence of mind to call for help in time to catch the angel, and he hung around for a while, not wanting to go back and face the fury of his many masters.

Ken didn't know what was happening but for once he wasn't in pain or abject terror. Instead of struggling or attempting to question his captor, he enjoyed the present and tried not to think about any horrors that the future might bring.

Not much later they arrived at their destination and Ken was deposited on the sofa. He felt as if he were back in his human body, but when he attempted to touch his own arm, there was nothing there. Ron and Claire knew there was a presence on the sofa by the grey light shining from it, and Gabriella explained that her mission had been a success. Ron disregarded the fact that Ken had been in hell and suffered terribly. He remembered how his own daughter had been as a teenager and was furious with Ken for the distress and suffering he'd caused.

'You bastard! How could you?'

'Ron, is that you? Oh Jesus, a friendly voice. You don't know how good it is to hear you, mate. You wouldn't believe what I've been through.'

'Trust me, I would and you deserved most of it, you bastard.'

The clouds in front of Ken disappeared and he could see his former colleague along with Gabriella and

Claire. He could also see that Ron was furious and was keen to tell him his side of the story.

'It just happened, Ron, honestly. We didn't mean to hurt you and Val finished with me before I died. And anyway,' they could hear the pleading in his voice. 'Isn't having my life cut short and all the horrible things that have happened since then punishment enough?'

'Oh sweet Jesus!' whispered Claire, realising that Ken had misunderstood the reason for Ron's anger.

The confusion cleared from Ron's face as the truth slowly dawned.

'You and Val? You. And. My. Wife!' Ron had turned a bright red and Claire expected steam to come out of his head.

'You didn't know,' mumbled Ken as he prepared himself for the onslaught.

Ron closed his eyes and clenched his fists. They could see that he was trying to control himself and Gabriella decided that it wasn't yet time to intervene.

'So this is why she felt guilty, because she had an affair with the scumbag who traffics innocent young girls.' He started beating his fists against his thighs in agitation. 'Why?'

Claire had never seen Ron so angry and upset. She moved to his side as a mark of solidarity and put her hand on his arm hoping to both comfort and restrain him if necessary.'

'Answer my question,' demanded Ron.

'I know I was a selfish bastard and I'm sorry, Ron. You'll never know how sorry. If there's anything I can do to make it up to you, trust me I will.'

'Trust you, trust you,' Ron blustered. 'How can you ask me to trust...'

'What about the girls?' Claire folded her arms and looked directly at where the dim light was starting to take the ghostly form of Ken's former human self.

'Ah. Pathetic as it now sounds, it was a good little earner.'

'So, motivated by lack of conscience and pure greed? I can't listen to any more of this lowlife's excuses.' Claire started to walk away but Gabriella called her back.

'I've changed my mind, Gabriella. Can you send him back?' Ron was back in control and folded his arms over his chest. Claire nodded in agreement.

'It doesn't work like that I'm afraid.' Her look silenced their protests and she turned to Ken. 'You may have the opportunity to redeem yourself, Kenneth. Would you like that?'

Ken looked at the angel and nodded eagerly.

He's like an excited dog that's been told it's time for walkies, thought Claire.

'In the meantime, get used to your new surroundings and I'll leave you to get re-acquainted with Ron and to get to know Claire.' She whooshed away and left the three to their own devices. An awkward silence filled the air with Ken wondering if he'd ever stop paying for his wickedness, Ron still furious with his former friend, and Claire pondering whether souls could actually kill each other.

*****

Graham and Carol had been called to Mel's school. The Head Teacher had phoned them both and said that it was a matter of urgency, but that she was unable to explain until they were face to face. Carol had contacted Graham and they'd agreed to meet in the school's public car park outside the main gates, and to put on a show of solidarity for the sake of their daughter. Graham waited in his car and his ex-partner showed up within two minutes of his arrival. It was the first time they'd seen each other since the acrimonious split and although awkward, this was put to one side because of the concern over their daughter.

'I wonder what she's done?' Carol was still angry with Graham and even being civil was a supreme effort.

'Why do you always assume that Mel's in the wrong? It might be something out of her control.'

'That's right. Your daughter is perfect and would never do anything wrong would she? Get real, Graham, she's a teenager and they experiment you know. It's all part of growing up.'

Carol slammed her car door. Her mouth was set and her eyes blazing. All the signs that she was spoiling for a fight thought Graham.

'Shall we get on?' Indicating with his arm that she should go first he smiled, trying to placate her and received a sneer for his efforts. They made their way up the hill to the school and the Head Teacher's office.

*****

Ken had answered Ron's questions as best as he could and had said sorry for the hundredth time. Ron was still feeling murderous and Claire couldn't stand the atmosphere any longer. 'Shall we go and see my brothers?'

Ron agreed, and when Ken asked if he could tag along, the looks he received in return answered his question. In case there was any doubt he was told to stay where he was until further instructions were received from Gabriella. He wasn't happy but knew he was in no position to argue and at least I'm not in pain thought Ken, knowing very well that his situation could be far worse.

*****

It was a workday and Tony was sitting on the toilet reading the newspaper before having his shower.

'I've got some information you may be interested in.'

'Jesus Christ, Claire. I'm in the bathroom. Can't you wait until I'm finished.'

'But this is important.'

'And so is this. You shouldn't sneak up on a bloke like that, you don't know what could happen.' It was so typical of his sister. When she was young and wanted one of them to help with something, she ignored their feelings and just barged into the bathroom or their bedrooms with total disregard for their privacy. Tony quickly finished what he was doing and had a rushed shower and shave.

'Is now convenient?' His sister's voice was inside his head as he was dressing.

'Could you just give me another five minutes?' he asked, knowing he was pushing his luck and Claire declined.

'The bottom line, Tony, is that I have details of our new sister's boarding school for you.'

'How did you...?'

'Never mind that. I can't give it to you until you've caught the muggers. Sorry.'

'Wait a minute.' Tony left the bathroom and called to his brother as he was getting dressed.

'Jim, Claire's here.' Jim rushed into Tony's bedroom and closed the door. 'Quiet for God's sake. Fiona doesn't know about all this yet.'

'Well. You're going to have to tell her,' said Claire, 'because she's a big part of our plan.'

'The plan to catch the muggers.' Tony explained to Jim and they listened while Claire said that she couldn't hand over the address of Mel's boarding school until the muggers were not a danger to anyone else. Her voice was in their heads and she was now able to communicate with both at the same time, as if she

137

were in the room talking to them. The twins got the wrong end of the stick.

'Are you under orders or something, Claire? Is this the only way we can get the address?'

This was a welcome distraction for Ron and he smiled. Her brothers had assumed that this was being imposed upon her and he nudged her and nodded frantically. Encouraging her to deceive them.

She wasn't prepared to lie outright but if they misinterpreted the information she gave them, so be it. 'Something like that, but let me tell you what I think you should do.'

She outlined the plan that she'd discussed with Ron. Fiona would frequent the street until the youths appeared and Tony and Jim would always be close behind but hidden from sight, so that she was never likely to be in true danger.

'The gang leader is scared of rats so if you take a rat with you, you can always use that if things don't go to plan.'

They laughed and Tony shook his head. 'I don't think we'll carry a rat with us thanks very much, Claire. In fact, I don't think we can help with this except for reporting them to the police.'

'Then when the police can't find any evidence and the muggers come up with alibis for the night of the attack, they'll release them and that won't do. If you do this my way, they'll be caught in the act and the three of you will be hailed as *have a go heroes.*' She declined to tell them that the people who'd saved Val from being raped had taken a photograph of the group leader.

'I can't put Fiona through that,' said Jim.

'Through what?' asked Fiona, opening the door and popping her head around it. 'And who were you talking to?'

138

Jim bit his bottom lip and Tony wouldn't make eye contact with her. They were both guilty of something, but Fiona wasn't sure of what.

'What's going on, Jim?'

'This will be interesting,' said Claire.

'Shut up, Cl...'

'No need for that, Tony.' Fiona's hands were on her hips and she thrust her head forward. 'What on Earth is going on?'

'I wasn't talking to you, Fi,' said Tony, and turned to his brother. 'How do we explain?'

'Try the truth,' said Claire, 'and see what she says.'

'Uh, huh.'

To Fiona, they appeared to be having a conversation with an invisible person. She was used to their weird twin telepathy and knew that was common with some twins, but this was all new to her.

'Right. You're freaking me out. Will one of you please explain?'

Jim took a deep breath and nodded. 'You're going to think we're nuts but Claire's talking to us.'

'Claire! As in your dead sister?'

'Yup.'

'You're right. I do think you're nuts.'

'Tell her I know she's wearing matching teal coloured underwear,' said Claire.

'Claire said to...'

'Not you, Jim, Tony.'

'I can't say that.'

'Yes you can. We have to make her believe you.'

'What the hell's going on?' Fiona felt like she was taking part in a farcical stage production.

'Err, Claire said to tell you she knows what colour underwear you're wearing,' said Tony, looking

139

anywhere around the room so that he didn't have to look directly at Fiona.

'And that would be?'

'Something called teal.'

Fiona looked at both brothers in turn. 'That could be the weird telepathy between you both.'

'Don't be ridiculous.' Jim was affronted. 'We don't do that sort of thing, we're not perverts.' He was mortified that Fiona would think that of him. 'Do you really think I'd do that?'

'The alternative is that your dead sister is in the room with us. Which do you expect me to believe? I'm out of here.' She left the room and slammed the door on the way out.

'That went well,' said Jim, and Claire told her brothers that she'd be in touch. She was keen to follow Fiona and make a mental note of some of her movements over the next few days. She'd then talk to her brothers again and this time they'd be able to convince Fiona that they were telling the truth.

*****

At the boarding school the gate guard passed their details to the security officer and he was now looking at his list on the millboard held in front of him, while Carol thought it would be easier trying to get into The Queen's bedroom at Buckingham Palace. They were eventually permitted entry following a call to the School Secretary and she now led the way into the Head Teacher's office.

Despite her name and incredibly posh voice, Mrs Chappleton-Myers was friendly and down to earth, though she did have an air of authority about her that encouraged good behaviour amongst both students and adults.

They were offered refreshments and waited patiently for the Head to explain the urgent nature of the visit.

140

'Melanie requested an appointment with me and she refused to speak with anyone else. She gave me some very distressing information.' She paused to ensure she had their complete attention. 'She told me that two of her friends have been coerced into performing unsavoury acts of a sexual nature, and have been threatened with violence if they report the information to the police.'

Graham realized that he had been holding his breath and he exhaled heavily. Carol shook her head in confusion.

'Is she all right?' Carol said what Graham was thinking and the Head nodded reassuringly.

'Melanie said that she didn't go with her friends when this happened. In that respect she's perfectly fine.'

'But why hasn't Mel spoken to me about this? She usually tells me everything.'

'It seems that Melanie is still annoyed at you for *'her whole life being one big lie'*. Your daughter's words I'm afraid, not mine.'

Graham coughed to fill the awkward silence, then asked. 'Are you absolutely sure she's all right?' The Head explained that Mel was upset because of the state her friends were in. 'I'm sure you understand that because of the seriousness of this information I had to go straight to the police. The problem is that the other girls have accused Mel of making it all up and now refuse to speak to her,' she shuffled some papers on her desk. 'When they were interviewed they denied any knowledge of Mel's story. The police say that the accused is known to them. He's been questioned and also denies the accusations. Mel has been cautioned for wasting police time but is still insistent that what she told me is the truth.'

'Mel isn't a liar,' said Carol. 'If she said something happened to her friends it's the truth.'

141

'Actually,' said the Head. 'I was wondering if it's anything to do with the change in your circumstances and perhaps she's attention seeking?'

Graham had heard enough. He stood up and approached the Head, putting both hands on her desk he leaned forward. 'Now look, Mrs Chappleton-Myers. If our daughter said something happened to her friends, then something happened. Did it not occur to you that the girls might be too frightened of the repercussions if they tell the truth?'

'Sit down, Mr Sylvester.'

Her tone took him back to his school days and Graham obeyed without question, despite the fact that he'd left school over thirty years before.

'Of course that occurred to me. But I've spoken to all concerned and the balance of probabilities leads me to believe that Melanie has at least exaggerated on this occasion. I've decided not to punish her this time but will be keeping a close eye on her behaviour in future. I've also asked her teachers to ensure that she's looked after and gets plenty of attention.'

'We need to speak to her,' said Carol turning to Graham. 'I'm worried.' It was the most civil she had been to him since their split and he would have smiled had it not been for the shared worry over their daughter.

'Melanie said she didn't want to see either of you,' she put up a hand to silence their protests, 'but I agree, you need to talk to your daughter. I'll take you to her.'

They walked along a quiet corridor in a section of the school not usually frequented by students, Graham assumed. The Head knocked and opened the door and they entered. The room was furnished with comfortable chairs, a sofa, television and a refreshment area. Mel sat on the sofa chewing a nail. She looked frightened, and forgetting about her daughter's

142

animosity, Carol held her arms out to her. Seeing her parents made Mel realize how much she'd missed them and she ran to her mother and they hugged. When they broke she looked at her father and he gave a tentative smile and opened his arms. Mel had by no means forgiven him but hugged him anyway. She felt a lot better now that her parents had arrived and addressed them both.

'I didn't lie, honestly.'

'Mr Moore,' said the Head, 'if you would, please.' She held the door open and followed Mr Moore through it, closing it quietly behind them.

They sat down and before her parents had a chance to ask any questions, Mel blurted out the whole story, including her decision to leave the taxi.

'I know you'll be annoyed and I shouldn't have got into it in the first place, but I wanted to show you I could do anything I wanted after what you two did to me.'

'Oh, sweetheart,' said Graham, 'I'm so sorry and I know I can't make it up to you but I thought,' he looked at Carol. 'We both thought that it would be better if you didn't know until you were older.'

'Well you were wrong.' Mel looked at her parents and temporarily forgot about her own situation for the moment. Seeing their expressions made her feel more like the adult than the child.

'I have to ask you this, Mel. But are you telling us the absolute truth?'

Back to being a teenager, she rolled her eyes then gave both parents a look filled with attitude. 'I knew you wouldn't believe me.' She folded her arms and looked out of the window.

'I'm not saying that we don't believe you,' said Carol, and her daughter looked directly at her.

'It's the whole truth. I obviously don't know exactly what happened at the so called party, but I do

143

know what Drew told me and that she's had nightmares ever since.'

They made some drinks and talked for a while longer.

'What happens now?' asked Mel.

'Well. We tell the Head that we know for a fact you're not lying. There's not a lot she can do though,' said Graham, 'if the police have already carried out an investigation and your friends won't tell the truth.'

'We'll take you home,' said Carol.

'But I don't want to go home, Mum. I haven't done anything wrong. And anyway, I don't want to get behind in my studies.'

What she'd said made sense but they were both worried about her.

'Are you sure about this?' Mel nodded at her father. There were only two weeks to half term and then they would see their daughter again.

'Would you like to come and stay with me for a few days at half-term?' He was desperate to put things right, 'then I can explain everything to you properly.'

'Can't you come and stay with us, Dad?'

'That's not a very good idea at the moment, Mel,' said Carol.

'Please, Mum. After all this I need you both.' She knew she could still get around both of them and so Carol reluctantly agreed that Graham could stay with them when Mel was home from school. She was sure she wouldn't need to explain that he would be in the spare room.

They hugged goodbye and the Head was along the corridor talking to Mr Moore when Carol opened the door. She made her way back to the room followed by Mel's Form Tutor. The visit was completed and the Head agreed that Mel shouldn't be taken out of school until the half-term break.

'Back to your class, Melanie, please.'

144

After she'd disappeared Graham and Carol insisted to the Head that their daughter had told the truth.

'I've explained my thoughts on the matter, Mr Sylvester, Mrs Dawkins. I think we should now focus on looking after Melanie so that she can concentrate on her studies.'

Neither parent pushed the matter further though Graham found it difficult to keep quiet. They didn't want to disrupt their daughter at such a crucial time in her education and she'd had enough upset due to their split. The visit was concluded and their thanks to the Head were luke-warm as they left and made their way back to the car park.

'What if she's in danger and what about her friends' parents? Do you think we should talk to them...' Carol was thinking out loud and firing the questions like a machine gun on automatic.

'Hang on, hang on.' Graham had considered the circumstances on the walk to the car park and although their concerns were the same, thought he'd come up with a few answers. 'Firstly, we both know how secure the school is. The Head has confirmed that Mel's confined to school grounds until half term. Secondly, the other parents believe their girls and not Mel. I think that if we talk to them it'll only make the situation worse. I'm hoping that they'll notice a change in their behaviour when they're home at half-term.'

Carol pulled at her bottom lip with her index finger and thumb as she tried to make sense of the situation.

'Okay, the school's safe and so is Mel for the time being. I would worry more if she were with you or me because we can't watch her for twenty-four hours every day. But when the truth does eventually come out, and I'm convinced that it will, none of them will be safe.'

'But the police will be involved then, Carol and they'll help. All this is really frustrating because they must know that she's telling the truth, especially if the guy involved has already got a criminal record.'

For the first time in ages they were able to talk without shouting at each other and they agreed the best way forward was to visit the police station and talk to someone in authority about their concerns.

*****

Claire had been busy following Fiona's movements and had missed her father's visit to her sister's school. She was currently in the cafe section on the fourth floor of a large department store. She looked around the trendy room approving of Fiona's taste. It had a black and white theme and offered designer sandwiches, beautifully presented tiny cakes and more varieties of coffee than the European Union had MEPs. The window table where Fiona sat had a stunning view of the city's panorama. Fiona was admiring the view when a voice turned her head.

'Kayleigh!' They hugged and Kayleigh joined her friend at the table. Ten minutes later with a tall, decaf cappuccino and latte in front of them, Fiona's strawberry concoction and Kayleigh's chocolate delight, they caught up with events since they'd last seen each other.

Claire was initially fascinated listening to their chatter about daily life. When the fascination turned to boredom she travelled around the cafe looking at some of the other clients and wondering what everyone was eating and drinking. When she'd been alive, shopping with Tash had been one of her favourite non-Jay experiences. Her time in the department store brought back many pleasant memories of when they'd been totally exhausted by the sheer effort of shopping for clothes and had flopped down gratefully in a cafe, surrounded by shopping bags and gagging for a cup of coffee. She floated along the queue of people waiting to be served and was disconcerted when a middle-aged woman in a navy blue business suit winked at her. Claire and Ron had always assumed that nobody could see them and were still shocked when the odd person was able to detect their presence. Gabriella had told them that although there were a lot of charlatans around who were happy to prey on people when they were at their most vulnerable, there were also a few people who could contact the spirit world and some who could see them but not talk to them. These were in addition to the angels sent to Earth by the Committee. Contrary to some beliefs there were far too many people for everyone to have their own guardian angel, but the angels did their best to help out when they could. She smiled shyly at the woman in acknowledgement and returned to Fiona's table.

As if on cue, Kayleigh put down her coffee mug and leaned in closer to her friend.

'So what's troubling you, Fi? Is it Jim?'

Fiona nodded. Kayleigh knew her so well and there was no point in denying it. 'Yes it is, but not in the way you think?'

'Sounds interesting.'

'Unbelievable and I know you're going to take the mickey, but please don't.'

Intrigued now, Kayleigh could hardly contain herself. 'For God's sake, Fi. What's happened?'

Fiona outlined the conversation she'd had with Jim and Tony in Tony's bedroom, and Kayleigh looked thoughtful. 'Hmm, it is hard to believe isn't it?'

'That's what I thought, until Tony mentioned the colour of my underwear and then I freaked.'

'So they're telling you that their dead sister is sending them messages?'

'Yup, and when I was listening outside the room, they were saying something about catching muggers and me helping.'

'Oh, I don't like the sound of that either.' Kayleigh saw the look on Fiona's face. 'Oh no, you're going to get involved aren't you? I can see it would be right up your street. Don't do it Fi.'

'The way I look at it, they were both very close to their sister and maybe this is their way of coping with her loss. I don't know about the other stuff but you know how I feel about Jim, and if he needs my help, well, what can I do?' She opened her hands, palms upwards, and shrugged, as if she had no say in the matter.

'The fact that you're an adrenaline junkie who craves excitement has got nothing to do with it of course?'

Fiona took a sip of coffee but the twinkle in her eyes was obvious to Kayleigh. 'So what are you going to do next?'

'I'll play it cool and wait for them to broach the subject. And as for the stuff with their sister, I'll try not to let it freak me out. I'm sure as time goes by that it'll happen less and less. I just have to remember that sometimes identical twins can be a bit weird.'

'But what if she's really visiting them and giving them messages,' said Kayleigh. 'Ooooh, the ghost of Claire Sylvester is watching you.' Kayleigh raised her arms and made ghostly noises and the two women burst into fits of laughter.

Bloody cheek, thought Claire, concentrating on one of the plates. She was as amazed as the two women when the chocolate delight plate crashed to the floor. Their laughter stopped abruptly and they looked around before gathering their bags and leaving the table, intent on more shopping but both spooked by the experience.

Chapter 11

Big Ed was not a happy man. He'd covered his tracks well and the police didn't have anything on him this time, but he knew what they were like. Only a stupid man would carry on with the venture and think he wouldn't be caught, and he certainly wasn't stupid. The parties had been a nice little earner and he'd lose face as well as money when he explained to the clients that they couldn't go on any longer. He could have sworn that the two girls wouldn't squeal, and this was confirmed when he'd contacted Alice and had a chat with her about her little brother. She'd caved in and eventually told him that it was the one who'd got out of the taxi. He recalled that her name was Mel, and she'd been to see her Head Teacher and that's what caused his current problems. Alice had insisted that she and Drew had not told Mel what they remembered from party and Big Ed believed her, for now. The girl Mel would need to learn that nobody messed with him. He'd have to be careful but would teach her a lesson she'd never forget.

*****

During the time she had followed her Claire had gathered plenty of information to prove to Fiona that she wasn't a figment of her brothers' imagination. It was a work night and Fiona was at the flat having dinner with the twins before Tony went out to give them a bit of privacy.

'Very tasty, Fi.' She'd made a quick pork stir-fry meal with egg noodles and it was absolutely delicious. They were chatting away about nothing in particular when Tony commented.

'Oh no.'

Fiona could see by the look on Jim's face that something weird was going on and she put down her fork.

'Is it your sister again?'

'It is and she says she smashed the plate. Does that mean anything to you?'

Fiona paled and Jim reached for her hand. 'Are you all right, sweetheart? You look like you're going to faint or something.'

'I'm fine, I'm fine.'

'She also said... I don't believe that I've got to tell you this,' said Tony cringing, 'but Claire said to tell you that a pink lipstick would suit you better than the dark red one you bought from Boots.'

Claire was satisfied to see that the look of disbelief on Fiona's face had now turned to one of resignation and acceptance.

Seeing that the twins weren't frightened by the strange presence gave Fiona confidence.

'Tell her I said she's a cheeky cow and that I'll help.' She smiled and now it was the twins' turn to be shocked.

'I heard some of your conversation last time she visited and it doesn't take a brain surgeon to work out that you need my help. This is still too freaky for me so I'm going to leave you to umm, talk to your sister or whatever it is that you do, then you can let me know what it is you need my help with.'

'She wants you to be bait so that we can catch muggers,' Tony blurted.

'Oh, wow!' Fiona walked to the door, 'bring it on boys.'

'And that's why I love that woman,' said Jim when Fiona left the room and thought she couldn't hear him. She felt lightheaded as she walked away, her lover's comment ringing pleasantly in her ears even though he hadn't yet said the magic words directly to her face.

*****

Ken had enjoyed the sanctuary of the sofa and had taken the time to reflect on events since his death. This had made him look back on his life with regret and something strange had happened to him. He realized that he did care and he wanted to do as many good deeds as they would allow him to prove to them that he could redeem himself. He wasn't yet sure if these feelings were borne out of fear for his future or genuine compassion and kindness. He also wasn't sure who the *they* were but knew that Gabriella was one of them. He hoped that he would be allowed to assist in catching the muggers. Thoughts of his immediate future induced a sense of urgency and a need to implement changes right away.

A whoosh followed by a dazzling bright light heralded Gabriella's arrival.

'Hello, Kenneth. How are you feeling?'

Ken was overcome with a joy he had never before experienced. He loved the being in front of him and not in the biblical sense. He would do anything to please her and at that precise moment in time, all he wanted was for Gabriella to be happy.

She had saved many deranged souls in her years as an angel and knew that he would be experiencing feelings of gratitude, love and blind adoration that he couldn't articulate.

'I'm happy and I want you to be happy, forever,' was the best Ken could manage and she gave him her most beatific smile, allowing him a moment of supreme peace and happiness.

'I want you to close your eyes and concentrate on what you feel right now.'

He did as instructed.

152

'The tasks I intend to bestow upon you will test you to your absolute limit. You will need to be able to harness that feeling and remember what it is like. It will be the one and only thing that can get you through some dark days ahead. Do you understand, Kenneth?'

He kept his eyes closed and tried to keep calm. The wonderful feeling was still with him and he never wanted it to go away.

'Are you sending me back to hell?'

A decision hadn't yet been made about his long-term future.

'No, Kenneth, I'm not. But I am giving you the best chance to redeem your soul and you will come up against some unforgiving opposition. You start by assisting Ron and Claire with whatever they need you to do.'

He opened his eyes and the moment had passed. 'When do I start?'

*****

Claire and Ron found themselves back in Cherussola. They hadn't made a conscious decision to return so understood that Gabriella had summoned them. Their instincts were correct and she told them to take a seat with Ken on the sofa.

'Things have calmed down somewhat and I now have a little more time on my hands. I'm going to be keeping my eyes on you and assessing your progress, Claire and Kenneth.'

'Excuse me, Gabriella. But you can't put me in the same category as...' Claire looked at Ken as if he'd crawled out of a sewer, '...him.'

Ken didn't like her tone or the look she gave him, but could understand her reasons, under the circumstances.

'Don't jump to conclusions, Claire, and be patient. I merely wanted you to be aware that I'm going to be about more to assist or intervene as necessary. I trust that your brothers and the plucky Fiona are willing to participate in your plan to catch the muggers?'

They hadn't told her about their plan so were surprised by her comments.

'A few of my assistants have been tracking your movements while I've been busy,' she explained. 'It's a risky strategy but I'm willing to let it go ahead. Ken will assist if you need him and I'll be about if things go awry.'

Ron and Claire looked at each other in confusion.

'Err, we weren't actually going to do anything, Gabriella. Claire's brothers and Fiona have agreed to set a trap and we were going to leave them to it.'

'Aren't you helping at all?'

'We're going to watch. The twins are perfectly capable of sorting out a few thugs,' said Claire, 'and Fiona is the sort of girl who can look after herself.'

'You can't ask them to do something this dangerous and not give them any back up. I insist that you are ready to be actively involved and prepare for the worst, even though it may not happen. Also be aware that all is often not what it seems, so keep your eyes peeled for the unusual.'

'What's that supposed to mean? Can you be more specific?'

But she'd disappeared with a whoosh, deciding to leave Claire's questions unanswered.

*****

Dressed in jeans, t-shirts and hoodies the twins left the underground station and starting walking to the address given to them by their dead sister. The further from the station, the more run-down the buildings appeared. The streets were unkempt with rubbish discarded on the ground, even though there were council rubbish bins liberally placed. The graffiti ranged from artistic to unimaginative with the worst about a girl named Elisha and what she'd done to certain parts of a Mikey's anatomy. There was also the usual nonsense about which was the best football team in the area. It had been a while since the twins had visited such a depressed location and they tried their best to look like part of the fabric and resisted the urge to stand and stare.

'I'm trying not to check my back every few seconds.'

Jim nodded in complete understanding with his brother. 'I feel sorry for some of the people born into this who don't have the motivation or education to drag themselves out.'

'Look out David Cameron. Jim Sylvester's coming to get you.'

'Me a politician?' he swaggered, 'I'm far too good looking for that.'

'And modest.' His brother laughed and they carried on walking in silence, each feeling an increased sense of tension as they neared their target's address.

They passed the block of flats where the guy named Mikey lived and tried not to be too obvious when looking at the building. They only needed to know how to get there and the lay of the land in case their plan went wrong and they failed to catch the attackers. About a four-minute walk in the same direction there were a few boarded-up shops and what looked like an old abandoned cafe. On closer inspection the cafe appeared to be open and the brothers decided to check it out.

The counter looked reasonably clean and the woman serving wasn't particularly friendly but she wasn't rude either. Having ordered tea and bacon butties both felt eyes burning into their backs. Tony turned around to face the potential aggressors. He folded his arms and his eyes swept the tables. He was well aware that they were in a dog eat dog location and he wanted the other customers to know that they were in the presence of pack leaders. Tony felt more like the runt of the litter but there was no way he intended to show that.

'What you looking at?' said a spotty youth with greasy hair, egged on by the other four sitting at his table.

'Fucking try me, sunshine!' Tony's pulse was racing like windscreen wipers in a rainstorm.

Jim turned and leaned against the counter. He folded his arms and hoped he looked menacing.

'Come on, lads,' said the woman behind the counter. 'I don't want any trouble.'

'Wanker.' This came from the boy at the table in an attempt to save face before turning back to his mates and deciding not to push Tony any further.

They moved to any empty table. Tony kept an eye on the spotty youth and Jim gave his brother a *what did you do that for* look as soon as he sat down with his back to their potential aggressors. When they finished they left the cafe, their unrushed attitude hiding the fact that they couldn't wait to get out of there. Eyes bore into their backs until they'd turned the corner of the street and Jim gave his brother a solid punch on the upper arm.

'Bloody idiot! What was all that about?'

'You know what these people are like,' Tony rubbed his sore arm. 'He was spoiling for a fight to impress his mates. I had to show him that we can handle ourselves.'

'And now they all know exactly what we look like.'

Tony disagreed. 'Didn't see their eyes, Jim? They were spaced out, the lot of them. They'll be lucky if they know what bloody day it is, never mind remembering a few strangers in a cafe.'

Jim hoped his brother was right as they carried on to their destination. A little later they turned a corner onto the street where Val was attacked. Despite it being broad daylight and most of the city streets were bustling with activity, this one was eerily quiet. It was a long side street in a location you would stumble upon if you had lost direction, and not somewhere you would purposely head for. There was nothing of interest there and it didn't appear to be a shortcut to anywhere in particular. There were a number of industrial sized rubbish bins placed right up against the dirty red brick wall which made the brothers think that a few food businesses might back on to the street, but otherwise nothing. There was a lamp at their end of the street and if they strained their eyes, they could see one more at the far end. The place would be very dark at night in between the lights and the brothers could understand why attackers would pick this location to carry out their heinous acts. Tony and Jim slowly made their way to the far end of the street trying to take in as much detail as possible while nobody else was about. They walked up and down twice until fully satisfied that they'd seen everything there was to see. On the second look, they decided to call it a day and noticed a pub on the corner. They entered and were pleasantly surprised to find that it was a decent looking place, and not a dive as they'd expected. Most of the other punters were dressed in business suits, quietly working on their laptops or with their mobile phones stuck to their ears deep in conversation. The twins felt out of place until they noticed a few tourists, lost off the beaten track they assumed. The middle-aged barman looked them up and down and took their order of two pints of lager. He watched them surreptitiously while serving other customers. Having had a good look around the area they were satisfied with what they had to do and would formulate a plan when they met up with Fiona that evening.

*****

Big Ed had been simmering slowly since his interview with the police. Over three weeks had passed and he knew they were following him and recording his every move. It had taken a massive strength of will for him not to take action against the interfering teenager. Not usually a patient man, Big Ed knew that the only choice he had was to wait until the police lost interest in him and then he'd sort her out. He'd wanted to act before the half-term holidays but he was still being followed. Last time he'd been tipped off that the police were following him, they'd lasted less than two weeks and he'd hoped this time would be the same. Although extremely annoyed and frustrated that this hadn't been the case, the fact that the police were spending a great deal of their time and resources on him appealed to Big Ed's ego. This would show the seedy world in which he operated that he'd now made the big time. He had a plan and he'd already spoken to the one person he could trust to help him - she'd agreed as he knew she would. Like he'd given her a choice, he laughed to himself. He'd sent her to the school as a prospective new parent and she had reported back to him on completion of the visit. He'd reluctantly agreed that they'd have to wait until the summer holidays to ensure their chances of success, and this made him all the more determined to teach the little bitch a lesson she'd never forget.

Chapter 12

Tony and Jim were fed up, but not as much as Fiona. Three times they'd been to the street where Val was attacked and the result had been the same each time. They'd seen youngsters hanging around, but these paid no attention to them. Although they were mucking about like kids do they didn't seem to be thugs or troublemakers. By the time the fourth Friday had come around they were merely going through the motions and had relaxed their guard considerably.

Fiona was about halfway down the dark street when she froze. Three shapes appeared out of the shadows and she could just make out another two lurking in the background. *Shit*, she thought, hoping that Jim and Tony had also seen them.

The twins had kept their distance and were about to turn the street corner to follow Fiona when three youths seemed to appear out of nowhere, one of them brandishing a knife.

'Give me your wallet, fuckwit,' said the one with the knife, the weapon and whatever he'd been taking making him feel brave. Tony recognized him as the spotty youth from the cafe but the boy didn't show any recognition of the twins.

'Don't be stupid. Get out of our way.' Tony didn't want to get into anything with the three that would mean they couldn't keep their eyes on Fiona.

Jim was starting to get agitated because Fiona wasn't in sight, but the youth misread his nervousness for fear and this spurred him on. His next move was written all over his face and Tony dodged the knife. The attacker didn't see the punch coming from Jim and screamed as he hit the deck. The others knew they were outclassed and ran away in the opposite direction. Jim grabbed the knife from the floor and Tony picked up

159

the youth who was visibly shaking. He threw him against the wall.

'You ever try something like that again, sunshine, and I'll break every bone in your body. Understand?'

The youth nodded as much as he was able to with a hand holding him by his neck.

'Now piss off and go back to your scumbag mates.'

He didn't need to be told twice and limped off as fast as his injuries would allow.

'Come on,' said Jim binning the knife as they hurried to find Fiona.

Fiona lowered her head and carried on walking, removing her mobile from her pocket as she did so. Where the hell were they? She thought they were all behind her, but she was wrong. The two who had been in the background had somehow passed her and now appeared in front.

'All right, darling?' They had smirks on their faces and Fiona felt the presence of the other three behind her.

'Just let me pass please and I'll be fine.'

'Now that wouldn't be any fun, would it?' came a voice from behind and she half turned so that she could see all five of them. Predictably, the one who spoke carried a knife and was throwing it back and forth between each hand.

'Do as I tell you, there's a good girl, and it'll be over quickly.'

Fiona didn't have time to answer before they all heard footsteps and saw the twins running towards them. Mikey knew they outnumbered the two guys but could see that they looked pretty fit. He panicked and as the twins neared and Fiona was watching them, grabbed her from behind and threw an arm around her neck. When the twins arrived on the scene Mikey held Fiona with one hand and held the knife against her neck with the other. His gang didn't like the look of the twins and two of them disappeared into the shadows like snakes into the undergrowth. His two closer foot soldiers remained, their eyes flitting from Mikey and Fiona to the twins in obvious agitation.

'They can't do anything while I've got her,' he said to reassure his mates. 'Jack their wallets.'

'I don't know what your problem is and why you've been hanging around in my territory, so I'm teaching you a lesson, innit.'

Jim took a step towards them and Mikey nicked Fiona with the blade. The blood seeped out of the left-hand side of her neck. Up until then she'd assumed it was all bravado, but now she was frightened and kept as still as she possibly could.

'Mikey, let's get back to the yard,' said one of the others as Jim and Tony reluctantly handed over their wallets.

Mikey felt a strange surge of power and didn't want it to end. 'Relax, man. There's nobody else about. Live a little.' He put his lips to Fiona's ear and pressed the knife harder to her neck. 'You want a proper man, darling.'

Jim knew that with his brother, they could take out the other two. He also knew that by the time they did Fiona could be badly injured or even worse. He sensed the leader was going to do something stupid and knew they were running out of time. He had to stop the guy before he could hurt her even more and knew that his only chance was to charge him. It wasn't usual for Jim to be indecisive, but when it came to putting the woman he loved in danger, he was hesitant. Mikey could see his indecision and was enjoying the game.

161

Gabriella had summoned Ron, Claire and Ken and they were all watching events unfold.

'Right, I've seen enough.' She flapped her wings as if limbering up, 'Time to help out.'

'What do you want us to do?' But she was on her way before she'd answered Ron's question.

Gabriella thought she'd left it too late, and when she saw that the youth was about to cut Fiona again, gave a quick nod to Ken. He swarmed towards Mikey, not knowing what to do but keen to help. He was stopped in his tracks by a dog. Not any ordinary pet, but a cur sent by the devil's messengers. Having had many different guises himself, Ken knew that the dog had once been human. The knowledge didn't do him any good as the miserable animal stopped his advance and threw him back against the wall. He slid down it, completely immobile and powerless to assist further. Ron didn't wait to be told by Gabriella and advanced towards the dog, slowly but purposefully.

Claire could see that her brothers were distressed and were trying to find a way to remove Fiona from her current predicament. She tried with all her might to communicate with them but their stress had closed the channel and her efforts were futile.

The dog recognized Ron as the one he'd beaten up when Mikey and his crew had attacked Ron's wife. He also recognized Gabriella as the angel who had stopped him from holding onto Ken and the one responsible for his current incarnation. Since the time he'd eventually returned to the devil's servants they'd made his existence a misery, and now he was determined that she should pay. He had to get past Ron first and Ron summoned every ounce of concentration so that Gabriella could save Fiona.

Mikey turned the knife so that the blade tip was at Fiona's throat. She felt his arm tense and closed her eyes, awaiting the inevitable. She felt as if her heart would burst through her chest and bizarrely, her mind took her back to when she was a child and had picked up a wounded sparrow. She remembered the bird's heart racing the same way that hers was now. The bird had died and Fiona now felt that her fate was to be the same. Powerless to act, she waited.

Gabriella hated changing form but she didn't have the time to consider other options. Mikey was about to cross the line and seriously injure his victim. He was sweating but with excitement, rather than fear. He wanted to take a final look at his audience to ensure he had their attention. His father said he'd never make anything of himself but Mikey would show him and the two freaks who looked like copies of each other. Two of his crew were watching and as soon as he'd done this and got away, his fame would be legendary. He could feel her trembling and instead of showing compassion, it gave him confidence and made him feel powerful. Milking the moment, he lifted his head slowly and the sick smile that had started to form on his face disappeared in a flash.

The rodent was big and grey and its eyes seemed to look right into his inner being. The rat's tail was swinging back and forth as if it had a mind of its own. The sight of it reduced Mikey to a gibbering wreck. Fiona felt his grip slacken and instinctively pushed his arm away. Jim was at her side in a nano-second and Tony was about to throw a punch when he stopped his arm in mid-air. The rat had sunk its teeth into the youth's shoulder and Mikey, screaming in agony and fear, sank to the ground hugging himself, the knife now a distance away and forgotten.

'Are you a man or a mouse?' asked Jim and Mikey squeaked in reply. 'Don't let it come near me again, man.' His shaking was so bad he looked like he was having a fit.

163

Tony shook his head and although he despised the youth and would have loved to give him a good beating, felt unable to do so when presented with the pathetic specimen on the floor in front of him.

Fiona had no such misgivings and her fear was replaced by blind rage.

'How dare you, you weak, selfish, pathetic excuse for a human being!' Each word was accompanied by a kick, and by this stage Mikey was screaming for her and the rat to go away. It took both Tony and Jim to pull her off and when she calmed down, her anger was replaced by tears. Jim held her while she sobbed.

Claire looked at the rat as it retreated to a corner and noticed something familiar in its eyes. Trying to work out why, she realized that Gabriella hadn't appeared for a while and the penny dropped. As she formulated her thoughts, a shadow flew past her toward the rat and she knew the evil dog was out for destruction. Claire willed the dog off course and at the last second the animal hit the wall next to the rat. She was almost as surprised as the dog. The stunned animal shook itself and weaved slowly away, staggering like a drunk after a Friday night out. The rat winked and remembering what Gabriella had said, Claire knew that she'd been right to intervene. This was confirmed when the rat changed shape before their eyes, and Gabriella re-appeared.

The other boys and evil dog now gone, Ron and Claire turned their attention to Ken. Although Ron still couldn't stand the sight of him, he was able to detach from his emotions and do the decent thing. They lifted him and knew that it would be some time before Ken would come round. Claire could see that her brothers were busy consoling Fiona and she resisted the urge to talk to them, deciding to give them space.

A light diverted everybody's attention. Tony, Jim and Fiona couldn't quite believe that the sun appeared to be in the street with them. It was different for Mikey. He felt himself burning from the bright light and tried to cover his face. The animals had disappeared and one moment the light was there, the next it was gone. The twins and Fiona smiled inanely at each other. After their experience they should have been traumatised and stressed. Instead, all they felt at that moment was peculiar warmth and a strange sense of wonder at the shining light.

'Do you think it was Claire?' asked Fiona, and Gabriella laughed to herself as she travelled back home, shouting, 'It was me...' knowing as she called that the living wouldn't hear.

Although not permitted to do it very often she loved the occasional light show, knowing how good it made people feel.

The twins shrugged and looked at Mikey, their awe at the light slowly being replaced by anger at the youth, and at what could have been. His face and hands looked burnt and, wondering what they'd witnessed, they put it down to intervention by Claire.

'I'll phone the police,' said Tony, and made a citizen's arrest after the call. Jim held Fiona as a number of emotions surged through him. They shouldn't have used her as bait and he intended to make it up to her. The realization that he may have lost her brought home his true feelings and Jim knew that this was the woman he wanted to spend the rest of his life with. He felt elated but vulnerable.

'I really love you.' Though upset at her ordeal, Fiona was over the moon that her boyfriend had chosen to tell her this for the first time in their relationship.

*****

'That's your phone,' called Val, her rubber gloved hands deep in the sink, washing the dinner dishes.

Marion answered. 'It's Tony,' she mouthed to her friend. She listened and nodded, frowning and looking worried at first, noted Val, but the concern was soon replaced by a big smile. Val could see that Marion was anxious to get off her phone to relay whatever she was being told. She took her hands out of the sink and removed the gloves, extremely interested in the conversation.

'What is it?' Val whispered, but Marion put a finger to her lips and said, 'Shhh,' as she listened to her son. After what seemed like an age later to Val, Marion said goodbye to Tony and put down her phone. Val had slowly been getting back to her old self, the only obstacle to full recovery being the knowledge that her attackers were still at large. Marion knew her news would put paid to that.

She locked eyes with Val and her friend already knew by the look on her face.

'They've caught them,' she said simply before they screamed at each other with delight and danced around the living room like a pair of lottery jackpot winners.

Four days later and Marion showed Val the newspaper report. The *Have a go Heroes* were featured with a photograph of the twins and Fiona posing in the middle in Charlie's Angels type stance. Marion was inordinately proud of her boys and Val would be eternally grateful to them. She'd already taken them out to dinner to thank them, and as it was the summer holidays, Carl and Libby had joined them. It was something else that bonded the two families together and both Val and Marion were hoping that the attraction between Libby and Tony would further cement this bond. The following week was the first anniversary of Claire and Ron's death and both women would need the support of each other to get through the day.

*****

It had been a difficult day, as they'd expected. Claire's ashes were in the memorial garden in her home town in Yorkshire and Marion had decided not to visit. After all, her daughter was in her heart and her head and she took the memory of her wherever she went. The fact that she knew Claire was fine on the other side didn't stop Marion's heart from aching with sadness at her daughter's death and she still missed her like crazy. They spent the morning looking at photographs, exchanging stories and crying. Both sets of children had called to check on their mothers and the conversations had been very tearful. By midday they both felt emotionally drained and the walls of the house seemed to be closing in.

'You know what. I'm sure Ron wouldn't have wanted me to mope around the house.'

'Claire would have said the same. She was too young, Val and she'd tell me to get on with my life.'

'Shall we go out for a while?' asked Val. She'd scattered Ron's ashes from a cliff top onto the sea in Brighton. It would take less than two hours for them to get there if they left now and the sea air would do them the world of good.

*****

When Claire had first discovered her mother talked to her every night, she visited as often as she could and it had been a comfort knowing how much she'd been loved. Over the last few months she'd felt a change in herself and knew that although she'd always love her family, it was time to move on. It was with these thoughts that Claire visited on the anniversary of her death. She would have loved to talk to her mother

167

the way she could with her brothers, but Gabriella told her that further messages weren't possible. She would have thanked her for all the wonderful times that built the memories of her childhood, for the unconditional love, and for not spoiling her too much, though at the time Claire would have preferred to have been spoiled. A year ago she would also have apologized for not being the daughter she thought her mother wanted. Now, having listened to Marion, she knew she was exactly the daughter her mother had wanted her to be, and wherever she ended up she'd be able to take that with her and cherish the thought. Marion was in bed when Claire popped in. She was in the middle of telling her daughter about her morning and how they'd decided to go to Brighton.

'We had a lovely afternoon, Claire. Fish and chips, and lots of people watching. We had a laugh when a seagull took a man's ice-cream cone when he wasn't paying attention. It made us both feel a little better. I hope you don't mind that I enjoyed myself a bit, even though it's the anniversary of the worst day of my life.' With that, she started crying and Claire had to wait for her mother to compose herself before she could continue.

'There's a massive hole that used to be filled by you. And whatever I do, it'll always be there, but I have to get on with my life. Now that I know you're going to be fine I hope you understand?'

Claire did understand and was glad her mother had changed over the past year. She now knew she could look after herself and would be able to cope with whatever life threw at her. Claire wanted to see how Jay had coped so blew a whisper of a kiss to her mother and said goodbye.

Marion said goodnight to her daughter. She thought she felt lips on her cheek and smiled to herself. She wasn't sure whether it was wishful thinking, hoping that Claire was there with her, but it made life slightly more bearable believing that. She surrendered her body to sleep, the only time that she didn't have to fight to put on a brave face and where she could dream that her beautiful girl was still alive and well.

*****

Jay had thrown himself into his work as an assistant chef at his uncle's hotel. It was easier to come home from work too shattered to think about how things could have been. He would finish his shift eat some food and catch up with a few mates on Facebook, just so they didn't get too concerned about him and preach to him that it was about time he moved on with his life. Then he'd fall into bed exhausted and sleep a dreamless sleep. Occasionally he would wake and forget she was dead. Although these days were becoming less and less, when they happened and realization hit, the pain was still like a cannon ball striking his guts.

He'd decided to take time off for the anniversary of Claire's death and to give the day the respect it deserved. Jay had moped around all day, looked at photographs, sniffed the old jumper of his that she used to wear and he hadn't yet washed, and cried enough tears to sink a ship. By the time the evening came around he'd reached a realization that he was actually ready to move on with his life. This came as a shock and he felt guilty for the unexpected feeling. He wasn't ready to think things through and was sick of his own company, so he showered and dressed in jeans, polo shirt and jacket and made his way to the pub.

Claire had paid a brief visit to her father. He'd met up with Mel for a few hours and had returned to his flat to change before going to visit the twins for a few days. Although her father didn't speak to her he'd opened a box that contained photos, a lock of her baby hair, and a few pieces of costume jewellery that she'd left at home before moving away. Graham had looked through the items, picking each one up and examining them intently, before placing them on his bed. When he'd found his most recent photo of Claire he held it to his heart and closed his eyes. The tears came then and Graham sat holding the photo to himself until he could cry no more. He returned the items to the box and put the box on a shelf in his wardrobe.

Visiting her parents had been emotionally draining for Claire and she decided she needed to rest and gather her strength before going to see Jay.

As soon as Claire was away the wedding fantasy appeared and she was at the part when the bride was about to walk down the red carpet. When she went to lock eyes with Jay something strange happened. She was viewing the scene from behind the seated guests and nodding her head in approval as Jay's bride, a short, slim, blonde girl, walked towards her groom. Claire was crying, but also smiling and clapping as she did so. Jay glanced her way, his look a question.

'Go ahead,' she said, 'she's right for you.'

Claire sat up in shock. She was now fully alert and Ron was in front of her. He must have sensed her distress as his face was full of concern.

'Not your wedding fantasy?' She'd told him that was the only one she'd had and he couldn't work out why she looked so shocked.

'Yes, but I wasn't the bride! It was someone completely different and not Jay's type at all,' she hesitated to recollect the vision. 'But I was happy for them both, Ron. He looked directly at me and I told him that she was right for him and to go ahead. I gave him approval to marry someone else.' She leaned back against the sofa, not yet understanding her feelings.

Ron sat next to her and held her hands in his. 'You've given him permission to move on. You still love him but want the best for him. That's the most wonderful thing you could do, Claire. I'm so proud of you.'

'But I still miss him so much.' Her eyes filled with tears and Ron couldn't find any words that would make her feel better. A hug was the best he could do, so he held her until she was ready to move.

'I want to see him; to see how he's coped today.'

Ron agreed, and they moved silently and quickly to visit Jay.

Claire had expected to arrive at his flat and was surprised when they found themselves in a pub. It was full of twenty-somethings and not a place they'd frequented together. She looked around and saw him with a crowd of people. He looked sombre but laughed occasionally. Claire noticed that two of the guys he worked with were keeping an eye on him and she was grateful for that. One of the women in the group was making sure that Jay knew she fancied him. He was uncomfortable with her flirting and Ron and Claire laughed when her body language became so obvious that she might as well have had *take me* written in large letters on her forehead. Fed-up with getting nowhere the girl, Kay, got up from her seat, gave her long auburn hair a shake to ensure that she had the attention of all the males at the table, and made her way to the ladies, wiggling her behind in exaggerated movements to get the interest of all the men she passed. It was wasted on Jay. One of the cubicles was locked and Kay folded her arms and talked to the door. 'Well, all I can say is that he must be gay.'

'So, because he didn't fall for your charms and you can't wrap him around your little finger, you think he's gay?' said the voice on the other side of the door and Kay heard the noise of the chain flushing.

171

'That's incredibly vain and small-minded.' The door opened and the short, pretty blonde girl walked out. 'You have to remember that the girl he was going to marry died in a tragic accident a year ago,' she said as she dried her hands and shook her head at her friend. 'Sometimes, Kay, you can be so insensitive.'

Suitably chastised, Kay followed her friend back to their table.

'Well, you're incredibly quiet for once.' said Ron. 'What's up?'

'That was her, the girl in the wedding dress.' Ron was slow to catch on, so she explained. 'The pretty blonde girl was the one I saw at the wedding ceremony. I think they're going to get married.'

Chapter 13

Val and Marion were preparing for their trip to Zambia. This was an extended project and they would be there for six months initially, after which they would have a two-week break and a decision would be made as to whether they would return. It was a few days before the flight and they were both excited and nervous. They had a final briefing to attend at the People Against Poverty HQ and Marion was concerned that the bad memories of the attack might be too much for her friend.

'I'm okay you know,' Val reassured. 'I need to exorcise the ghosts so we should go out for the evening after the briefing.'

'Are you joking? Talk about tempting fate.'

Val laughed at her friend's raised eyebrows and open mouth. 'I'm sorry, Marion. It's something I've got to do. You don't have to come with me though if you don't want to.' Val held her breath for a moment and was relieved when Marion answered.

'Are you insane? Of course I'll come with you.'

Claire, Ron and Ken watched as Val and Marion returned to the scene of the attack.

'Last time I saw Val was the night I died. I tried calling for help but the words wouldn't come.' Ken was talking almost to himself and didn't pick up on the negative vibes from Ron who was doing his best not to listen.

'I don't think Ron wants to know about the circumstances of your death, especially as you were with his wife you insensitive bastard!'

'Thanks, Claire.' Ron hid a snigger. Her honesty and loyalty had certainly lightened his mood and had Ken been a dog he would now be running down the street with his tail between his legs.

Val's deceit had obliterated Ron's faith in the human condition and he'd tried his best to hate her. It was a fruitless exercise. He'd now forgiven her totally - partly because it was obvious to him that her guilt had almost destroyed her and he could see that she was genuinely sorry. She carried her guilt around with her every day but he hoped that the charity work would make her feel better about herself.

It wasn't yet dark and although Ron was concerned for his wife, he also knew that it was something she had to do. The evil spirit youth decided to put in an appearance, this time in his former human guise. He'd called for assistance from his brothers of evil but none had been forthcoming. The trio were unprepared for a fight and relieved that no more evil spirits were in attendance. The dead youth watched, assessing his chances as the two women walked along the street. Outnumbered and too cowardly to start his own trouble he soon disappeared to find havoc elsewhere.

It was as if it was happening all over again. Val remembered how she'd felt on that night and wondered if the attack was really her punishment for being unfaithful to Ron and for the circumstances surrounding Ken's death.

'If only I'd stayed in with you. If only I hadn't...'

Marion squeezed her hand and interrupted. 'Life's full of '*if onlys*', Val. We can't change any of them so no point in trying, you'd drive yourself nuts.'

If only she hadn't had an affair. If only she hadn't gone out that night. If only Ron hadn't agreed to work nights. If only...

'Ready to move on?' Marion's words brought her back to the present. One day she might tell her friend the whole story.

'In more ways than one,' Val gave a sad smile. 'Shall we go to the pub?' She pointed to the pub on the corner and Marion nodded.

'Sure. Are you all right?'

'Better than I thought, Marion. Let's go and get on with our new lives.'

The three spirits would have breathed a collective sigh of relief had they been able. Instead, they floated away, secure in the knowledge that the street was now safe and so were Ron's wife and Claire's mother.

They turned down offers of lifts from their children, deciding instead to meet them at the airport to say their farewells.

'It's a short train trip for us, and you know it's impossible to find a parking space.'

'And it costs a fortune,' added Val.

They were both surprised when Tony and Libby arrived together and the couple tried their best to ignore the knowing looks between their mothers. Carl was next to arrive, followed by Jim and Fiona.

'Shall we tell them?' said Fiona and Jim nudged her. They'd agreed not to gazump his mother's departure by telling her their good news. Fiona knew that Marion would be furious if she found out from someone else, and she was so excited that she wouldn't be able to keep it quiet for the six months that her future mother-in-law would be away.

Marion held her breath and crossed the fingers of her right hand behind her back.

'Mum, I've asked Fiona to marry...'

'And I said yes,' interrupted Fiona, too excited to keep quiet.

'Oh, that's fantastic.' The tears that the mothers had tried to hold back now came as if a dam had been opened and Fiona and Libby joined in while the men slapped Jim on the back, and the women kissed and hugged.

'You are going to wait until we come back aren't you?'

They laughed and Jim told his mother that the wedding Fiona wanted would take at least a year to plan.

'Hollywood blockbusters have smaller productions.'

'Ow, that hurt.'

'I haven't seen so many tears since our funerals.' Claire was beaming at her brother's good news. Ron turned away so she couldn't see him crying quietly. She had moved on from Jay and was slowly learning acceptance. He hadn't told her but he still felt unable to let go of Val and the need to look after her and make sure she was safe was as powerful as it had always been.

'We can still visit them in Zambia, you know. It's not as if we have to get flights,' she said without looking at him.

So she does understand, thought Ron as he watched Val and Marion wave to their children before disappearing through customs and onto the departure lounge.

*****

It had been an immense effort for Big Ed to keep out of trouble while the police were tracking his every move. As the months had passed slowly his annoyance about Mel reporting him turned into a beast with a mind of its own. His fury was a cold, hard

176

animal and he intended to take his revenge as soon as he was able.

It was the end of September when DI Sparks was called into his DCI's office. He was told that they had another 24 hours to find a scrap of solid evidence before being pulled out. Resources were tight and they had other investigations on which to spend the public's money.

Sandy hadn't heard from her lover for a while and wondered when he might turn up. Depending on his mood he could be scary or very loving, but always totally dominant. She looked at the caller ID when her phone rang and her heart skipped a beat. Hopefully nobody had upset him. She found it hard to cope when he punished her for events beyond her control but deep down she knew she deserved it. As soon as she heard his voice she breathed a sigh of relief. Big Ed was over the moon. He told her that the police had stopped following him a few weeks earlier and he'd left it this long just to be sure. They could go ahead with the plan. She was disappointed he didn't want to see her straight away and wasn't comfortable about his request. She'd promised ages ago that she'd help - thinking at the time that he wasn't really serious - and knew the consequences if she tried to change her mind. She'd backed herself into a corner and there was nowhere left to go. He'd been understandably impatient for the plan to go ahead at the spring half-term break, then the summer holidays, but the police had still been there like legal stalkers. Now, with one week before the schools broke up for autumn half term it was time for action. She put down the phone and looked up her notes on the girl's mother. Providing her routine hadn't changed Carol did her weekly shopping after she finished work on a Wednesday evening. This was perfect for Sandy and the following Wednesday she just happened to be in the same supermarket.

'I'm very sorry,' said Sandy as her trolley bumped into Carol's. 'Oooh, I just love that chocolate.' Sandy pointed to the chocolate that had been recently advertised on TV by a beautiful slim pop star who probably hadn't eaten chocolate since she'd reached puberty. Carol looked in her trolley and smiled. 'Hmmm, it's my weekly treat.'

'I'm off to get some now.'

And Carol watched as the strange-looking, nervy woman whose long fringe covered most of her face rushed off down the sweetie aisle. She finished her shopping and went home and watched her favourite soap. At the credits she quickly logged on to her computer and spent the next half hour messaging Mel. She was so looking forward to seeing her daughter and told her that she had a few surprises in store for her for half term. Mel sounded excited at the prospect and when they'd finished Carol turned in early, relaxed and contented. She had one of her rare nights when she slept well and woke up later than usual, refreshed and raring to go. Her long shower left her little time to get ready for work and it wasn't until lunchtime that she noticed her mobile phone was missing – by then it was too late.

*****

The school secretary answered the phone on the third ring. It was the penultimate day before half term and she was more than ready for the break. The Head was off on compassionate leave - her elderly mother had had a stroke and she had been understandably distressed. They didn't expect her to return until at least the beginning of November and her absence had increased the school secretary's workload. And now Carol Dawkins was on the phone saying that she knew it was short-notice, but that she wanted to

178

take Mel out of school that afternoon instead of the following as she'd booked a late deal holiday for her.

'I'll have to get permission from the Deputy Head, the Head is indefinitely indisposed.'

The voice on the other end of the phone said she'd trust that the school would be sympathetic after the difficult times that Mel had experienced. The secretary replied that she'd get back to her within the hour.

Mr Moore, Mel's form tutor, thought it was a marvellous idea and went to speak to the Deputy Head.

'I appreciate it's against school policy,' he said, 'but with the break-up of her parents, the revelation about her father's other family and also that business with the police, it's been a very difficult time for Mel Dawkins.'

Mr Lawson put his hands behind his back and looked out of the window. The sky was grey and he could see leaves dancing in the autumn wind. This pontificating wasn't getting him anywhere but he knew he had to think carefully before making the decision. Young Mr Moore couldn't be seen to have it all his own way.

'I can't emphasise enough how good a holiday would be for Mel,' he swallowed and added, 'it would really be appreciated if you could bend the rules on this occasion, I would say the circumstances in this case are exceptional.' Mr Moore smiled ingratiatingly, despising himself for doing so and hoping he was doing a good job of hiding his true feelings toward the Deputy Head. It didn't matter anyway as he was currently speaking to his back.

Mr Lawson turned. 'Very well, you've convinced me. But carry out the proper security checks first and ensure that nothing funny's going on. After that business earlier in the year, we don't want any scandals for the school.'

179

'Of course.' *Did he think he was stupid?* 'I'll make sure we do. And thanks.' His gratitude was genuine and he returned to the office to instruct the secretary to confirm the arrangements with Mel's mother. This was done in a hurry, as Mr Moore was keen to give the good news to his star pupil.

Mel was thrilled. Not only was she leaving school a day early but her mother was taking her on holiday. It was only for a week but she'd have a tan and would be the envy of all her friends on her return.

'I hope it's somewhere warm,' she said squeezing her arms together, 'I'm just about packed anyway so that won't take me long.' She was thinking out loud, Mr Moore forgotten in her excitement.

'Hmm. Mel?'

'Sorry, Sir.'

'Have you heard from your mother?' he asked, putting his thumb in his blazer pocket with the fingers outside, Prince Charles style.

'Can I check my phone?'

He nodded. The students were allowed to keep their phones on them but only permitted to use them during break and meal times.

Mel read the text and handed her phone over to her teacher.

'That's a little strange that she wants to pick you up from the garage in town and not the school?'

'Hmm, but it does say that we'll save half an hour if I can meet her where she's filling up the car, and the flight times are really tight.'

'Fair enough,' said her teacher. 'It's not as if she always picks you up from school.' Mel had met her mother in the town before, but with the Deputy Head's words still ringing in his head, he would get the secretary to call Mrs Dawkins to see if she could come to the school instead.

'Go on then, Mel. Go and get changed and get ready to go and come to the office at 2pm so we can sign you out.'

She nodded and tried not to run to her room, her mind whizzing with thoughts of sandy shores and good looking waiters. Her friends would be green. The only thing that slightly marred her happiness was the fact that she couldn't share it with Drew and Alice. Since their denial earlier in the year their friendship had suffered and she'd been moved to a different room. Although she'd made new friends, she missed them both, more so Drew who'd been taken out of school and nobody knew what was going on with her.

*****

The twins had discussed their half-sister with Fiona and Libby the night before. The girls thought it reasonable that they wanted to meet her, especially having lost Claire fourteen months previously.

'And your father says it's too soon to see her?' asked Libby.

'That's right. But I think it should be her choice.' Tony had left out the bit about their father asking her if she wanted to meet them and Mel saying that she didn't. Jim raised his eyebrows at his brother, but Tony decided to ignore him. Fiona didn't miss the look.

'And what does she think? She must have an opinion, surely?'

'Well what...'

'Who knows?' Tony interrupted his brother.

'Well I think you should arrange to see her, but only if she wants to see you both,' said Libby and Tony smiled and kissed her on the cheek. They'd been extremely patient with their father and he still hadn't arranged a meeting. Their curiosity had won over patience and the brothers planned to visit Mel's school the following day and hoped to see her when her mother picked her up, amongst the general chaos that went along with collection of hordes of children. They'd seen a few photos of Carol at their father's flat, one of her and her distinctive car, so it shouldn't be too difficult. Jim could see that Tony didn't intend to come clean with the girls. He hated deceiving Fiona so kept his head down in the hope that she wouldn't guess what they were up to. He didn't fancy an argument tonight, with his brother, or with his fiancée.

*****

The school secretary had said that Mel was definitely to meet her mother at the filling station so she was making her way there. She attempted to pick up her rucksack out of the luggage compartment of the bus. The other passengers smiled at the sight of the teenager trying to sling a bag almost as big at herself onto her back. A man felt sorry for her and got up to give her a hand and she took out her earphones and thanked him. He acknowledged the thanks, grateful that some of the day's youth had been brought up with manners and respect for their elders. She held onto the pole until the bus stopped, then grabbed onto the straps of her rucksack, hoisting the pack further up her back. She thanked the driver - impressing her earlier helper even more - and jumped off the bottom step. Mel put her earphones back in, planning to listen to her iPod for the ten-minute walk to the petrol station where she would meet her mother. She didn't get there and her mother didn't know she was missing until the following day.

*****

Carol was cursing herself for losing her phone. She'd hunted high and low but still couldn't find it. She knew that Mel wasn't expecting her to call today and that she'd be seeing her tomorrow, but was still miffed. She intended to turn the house upside down at the weekend and buy another if she couldn't find it. Mel

182

was always going on to her to buy a smart phone so she'd treat herself if her old pay as you go didn't turn up, and her daughter could help her choose it. She was about to log-on to her computer for a quick chat with Mel when she remembered that she had a hockey match and wouldn't be back yet. Tomorrow would come soon enough and they could have a proper face-to-face catch up.

*****

It took the twins ages to find a parking space.

Tony looked around. 'Most of these are abandoned and not parked. Bloody women drivers.'

'Don't let the girls hear you say that.'

They laughed and got out of the car. After a search of the car park, neither saw Carol's Nissan Micra. They got back into the car and waited, people-watching as the parents, mostly mothers, returned to the cars with their children, fussing over them as if they hadn't seen them for years and not weeks. It wasn't long before the little blue car with a flower and bee emblem on the passenger door arrived. The car park was now overflowing and they watched her park in the wooded area between two trees, the little car's wheels spinning on the muddy surface. Carol made her way to the path wiping the bottom of her shoes on the grass before walking on the stony surface.

'What now?' asked Jim, and Tony's look told him that they wait until she returned to the car with their sister.

'Should be less than fifteen minutes if the others are anything to go by.' And so they prepared for the short wait before getting the first look at their sister.

Fifteen minutes passed, then thirty. Both started to feel uneasy and as they were beginning to suspect that something wasn't right, a police car arrived carrying two uniformed officers who got out of their car and waited. Another car arrived shortly after and a

183

man and woman in plain clothes approached the uniformed officers. It seemed to the boys that they were giving them instructions and it was pretty obvious that these were plain clothed detectives.

'Come on, let's go in,' said Tony but Jim put a restraining hand on him.

Tony knew he was right - there was no way they could go and introduce themselves to their father's ex-lover when she was dealing with some sort of crisis over her daughter.

'We'll need to wait and see what happens but I'm going to call Dad.' He hung up when there was no answer and the twins remained in the car worried about their half-sister, each minute that ticked away seeming like an hour.

Tony was looking out of the window towards the trees. 'She's not there is she?'

Jim didn't need to say anything. They feared the worst and sat in silence, each lost in his own thoughts and undecided what to do next.

'Duck!'

Tony obeyed instantly, but it was too late as their father banged on the driver's side window. Jim sat up as if he'd been looking for something on the floor of the car and rolled down the window. The anguish showed on his father's face.

'Mel's gone missing.' He was rushed and agitated, stopping only briefly on his way to the school. He hadn't bothered quizzing them about their presence, nor had he asked how they had got the address or why they were trying to hide from him.

'Where is she? Is she safe?'

Graham shook his head, turning his back on their car as he made his way to the school building. 'I don't know the full story. Carol phoned me and she was frantic. Somebody called yesterday and pretended to be

184

Carol. I don't know any more. I'll contact you as soon as I do.'

'We'll wait here until you come out, Dad,' Tony shouted as they watched him hurrying away.

*****

Mel opened her eyes slowly and the room moved. She felt like she had when she'd tried too many Alco pops and she squeezed her eyes shut again before re-opening them. She vaguely recalled being grabbed from behind and not being able to move. Then something damp and smelly had covered her mouth and nose. She'd hoped it was a bad dream but now that the blurriness had gone and she sat up on the unclean mattress and looked around, she knew it was real. The room was bare, with damp rising from the floor and a sink in the corner. She didn't know what colour the walls had once been, they varied from a dirty grey to a gone off cream. There was a small window, which had bars on it, and it wasn't until she went to move from the bed to have a look out of the window, that she realized that her right hand was shackled to the side of the bed frame. She tried to quell her rising terror by allowing her anger to rise to the surface and she banged her free hand on the mattress.

Her stomach rumbled and Mel realized that she hadn't eaten for a while. She looked at her watch and saw it was 2 o'clock. She could see it was light outside so it must be the afternoon and it must also be Friday. So she'd slept for almost 24 hours, no wonder she felt so muggy. She was desperate for the loo and when she put her feet on the floor, one hit something. She looked and saw the cracked potty at her feet. After some internal wrangling, she decided to swallow her disgust and attempt to use the vessel – it was either that or wet herself. The shackle was long enough for her to be able to get off the bed and bend down. She could use her hand a little but had to wrap her left hand around the back of her body to pull down her underwear. Despite her circumstances it was a good feeling to be able to relieve herself. When she'd rearranged her clothing after she'd finished and sat back down on the bed, she contemplated her circumstances in an attempt to stop the terror from taking over.

Before Mel had time to think properly about the situation the door to the room opened. A woman dressed in a black gown from head to toe, with only a slit for her eyes, walked slowly into the room carrying a tray. Despite her own fear, Mel noticed that the woman walked with a laboured limp as if she were in pain.

'Stand and face the wall.' Mel followed her orders.

'Where am I? Wh..'

'Shut up,' said the voice in barely a whisper and she did as she was told.

The tray was placed on the mattress at the bottom of the bed and Mel saw the woman leave from the corner of her eye. She waited for the door to close and remained facing the wall for a few minutes before turning to sit down and face the tray. It contained sandwiches, a can of coke, a bag of crisps and an apple. Abduct me but make sure I have one of my five a day, thought Mel as she debated whether to eat the food, wondering if it might be drugged. Her hunger won and she devoured it as if she hadn't eaten for a week, not a single day. The food made her feel better initially, then the hours passed and all she could do was think.

There was no doubt in her mind as to who had arranged the abduction and she remembered how distressed Drew and Alice had been after their encounter. She tried being brave and hoping for the best but lost the battle. The fear crept into every fibre of her being and she lay down and curled into the foetal

186

position, crying and calling for her mother. Nobody heard her.

*****

DI Sparks left the school reassuring the parents that the police would do everything they could to find their daughter as soon as possible. The mother was beside herself and had reluctantly accepted comfort from the father but the DI didn't need to be told that they were no longer together. Years in the job had made him an expert on body language and subtle nuances of human behaviour, and he could see that the mother was resentful of the father. Mind you, he thought, anyone with an IQ of one or more would be able to tell that the ex-couple still had many issues.

He'd left his best Liaison Officer at the school and she'd be able to tease out any information from the parents and teachers without causing them further distress. He didn't yet have proof but his gut instinct told him that Big Ed was behind this although he'd been a relatively small time criminal previously. If he could get the teenagers to talk about the party earlier in the year, he'd be able to prove the connection and knew his boss would be one hundred per cent behind him. Back at the station he quickly briefed the DCI who authorized an All-Points Bulletin for Edward Cathcart, AKA Big Ed. DI Sparks also arranged interviews with the parents of Drew and Alice. Alice's parents were sympathetic but unhelpful and he was informed that they would get back to him after speaking to their daughter, and that on no account was he to attempt to speak to her before then. Even informing them about the danger Mel Sylvester was in elicited the same response, and DI Sparks left feeling frustrated and deflated. He'd called ahead to Drew's mother who'd told him to come round straight away. He felt slightly more positive as he knocked on the door accompanied by his detective sergeant.

She smiled a weary smile and stepped aside to let them into the house. A quick glance told him that this was an affluent family and she led him into the lounge. DI Sparks noticed the computer on in the study and a few files askew on the desk.

'I'm working from home for a while until Drew's well enough to go back to school,' she said, and he raised his eyebrows. 'Come and sit down and I'll explain.'

They accepted her offer of coffee and once she brought in the drinks, she explained,

'Drew's not well and is currently undergoing therapy.' They were the only people she'd told outside of her immediate family and she let out a deep sigh at the revelation. 'Her therapist believes that her self-harming is due to a traumatic event that she's not yet ready to talk about, but I'm beginning to think that Drew's friend was telling the truth. And now you say she's missing it doesn't take a genius to put two and two together.'

Bingo! They were getting somewhere. The mother agreed that they could interview Drew as long as her therapist could be present and events moved swiftly from that point. DS James rang the therapist and he cancelled his appointments for the remainder of the day and arrived at the house within thirty minutes.

Drew was still frightened, but upset when she heard that Mel was missing, knowing that if their suspicions were correct she could have prevented it. It was hard after keeping it in for so long but she told the police all that she could remember from the night of the party and her mother held her as she recalled what she could. Drew looked down and cried, feeling a mixture of shame and relief.

'Why, oh why didn't you tell me?' She held her daughter and stroked her hair, wishing she could make her pain go away.

'I'm sorry, Mum. I'm so sorry.'

The police and therapist remained silent while mother and daughter shut out the rest of the world for a few moments, Drew taking comfort from her confession at long last and from the love and warmth of her mother. The police reassured them that she would be safe. Now that the truth was out, the therapist knew that the healing process could start and the police left shortly after, telling Drew's mother that a family Liaison Officer would be allocated, and leaving DI Sparks' contact details should she need them.

He made various calls on the way back to the station and it wasn't long before he was able to have a chat with one of his snouts.

Chapter 14

Claire, Ron and Ken were waiting patiently for Gabriella. Ken was pacing back and forth and was extremely nervous in anticipation of his future. Gabriella had informed him that the Committee had decided to give him one final chance. He was to return to Earth for a rebirth. Although relieved that he'd escaped a future of hell, for now at least, he had mixed feelings about not being able to remember his latest life and his next one would be the only one he'd remember until his soul was sent to its final resting place. Ken was literally soul searching and hoped that he did really have a good side and that it would prevail, whatever his future life held in store. The sudden whoosh interrupted his thoughts and he closed his eyes for a few seconds to calm and prepare himself for what was to come.

Claire was the first to notice that all was not well. Instead of the usual serenity that accompanied Gabriella, she felt a sense of urgency and spoke before the others fully realized that something was up.

'What is it?'

'Very perceptive, Claire, you are progressing quite nicely,' she allowed herself a small smile before turning serious. 'But I have bad news.'

They waited and she looked at each in turn. 'Kenneth, your rebirth has been postponed, but don't worry, it will still go ahead.'

'What is it?' Claire asked again and Gabriella carried on as if she hadn't heard.

'The bad news concerns your new sibling, Claire. I'm afraid she's been abducted.' She waited for the information to sink in. 'And they're going to need help to rescue her.'

Claire put her hand to her mouth. She'd seen her sister on a visit with Ron, but didn't know her. Why then did she feel a sudden surge of love for the missing girl and an overwhelming need to find and protect her?

'I know, Claire. You do love her, but can't understand why. It happens and it's a perfectly normal reaction.'

Ron felt for his friend and gave her a comforting squeeze before asking how it happened.

'She was told that her mother was taking her out of school a day before they broke up, to take her on holiday. It was a ruse of course, and she was taken shortly after she left the bus.'

Gabriella explained how the woman pretending to be Carol had arranged for Mel to go into town.

'But why would the school allow that? What about security? And where have they taken her?'

'Questions, questions, questions, Claire. I don't know all the answers, yet. One of my staff was dealing with a soul and only saw the event in passing. He returned later to find out what had happened and reported back to me as soon as he could.'

'I bet it's Big Ed.' Ken had remained silent until then and Gabriella nodded in agreement.

'From the description I was given it appears so, and he has a female accomplice. Ron and Claire, I want you to go and help.'

'But what about me?'

'You will stay here, Kenneth, until I can reorganize my schedule and send you to your new life.'

'But what if Ron and Claire are still away when that happens? Will I see them again?'

The others tried to hide their surprise at his comments. It wasn't as if they were besties.

'Probably not. Well not for a good number of years hopefully, and only then if you prove acceptable to the Committee.'

Ron smiled, picking up the inference that they would only see him if he was good which meant that Claire's final place was heaven. It was totally lost on his friend who was deep in thought, considering her sister's circumstances he assumed.

'We don't know where the girl is and I want you two to find out and alert the authorities.'

'But how...'

'Use your initiative and your brothers of course, Claire. Now any further questions?'

They said nothing as she hadn't answered the questions they'd already asked.

'Good. Start at Big Ed's location and see where that takes you. Goodbye and good luck.' She disappeared and they quickly said their goodbyes to Ken and disappeared themselves. He was left as he was before she'd arrived, contemplating his future life, but also regretting ever meeting Big Ed.

*****

Roger missed the parties but all thoughts of the good times disappeared as he listened to the news headlines. He broke out into a cold sweat. With hand shaking he removed a red spotted handkerchief from the breast pocket of his suit and wiped his forehead. He picked up his phone to make a call but slammed it down as his secretary walked into his office.

'What is it?'

'You said to come in for a diary check at 2pm and it's ten past now,' she smiled patiently as if talking to a child.

'Can't you see I'm busy. We'll do it later.'

'Okay. Would you like a coffee?'

'Just get out and leave me alone.'

'Certainly.' That was rude even by his standards and she noticed that he did look more stressed than usual. She smiled again and left the office, wondering if his wife had at long last found out that he was up to something. She didn't know exactly what, but she did know that he had something to hide and suspected that it was both immoral and illegal.

Roger locked the door before picking up the phone and calling his three friends. They had the same reaction as him when they heard that a girl had gone missing and that the police were looking for someone fitting Edward Cathcart's description. As Roger hung up there was a knock at the door.

'Piss off!' Stupid cow, how many times did he have to tell her he didn't want to be disturbed?

'It's the police, Mr Lancaster. Open the door now or we'll open it for you.'

Roger looked around, desperately. Jump out of the tenth floor window or open up to the police. It was a no brainer. He opened the door and glared at his secretary as if she were the cause of all his problems.

'We need to talk to you as a matter of urgency,' said DI Sparks after showing his ID. 'Get your coat, we're going to the Station.' And Roger cursed the day he'd met Big Ed.

*****

Mel was struggling to breathe and it was this that woke her. It was pitch dark and she felt pressure on her throat. Still groggy from sleep, she shook her head trying to move then lifted her free hand realizing that someone was squeezing her throat. She attempted to remove the hand that was causing her pain. It was a vice-like grip and it didn't budge. It didn't occur to her that this might be the end and she thrashed about as much as she was able trying to break free. Suddenly, the hand moved of its own volition and a light was turned on, almost blinding her. Her eyes adjusted to the

193

light some seconds later and she took in a sharp intake of breath when she at last recognized the face in front of her.

He leaned toward her, his face inches from hers and Mel turned her head to face away from him. He squeezed her cheeks, forcing her to face him. He smelled of stale tobacco and what she thought was whisky, combined with a sickly sweet mixture of sweat and too much aftershave lotion. She coughed and tried not to gag.

'I'm arranging a little party for you. And you'll be sorry. I'm saving you for them but I might have a go after they've finished.' He gave her face a little slap and smiled. That was all he said before getting up from the bed and walking to the door. He winked and left the room.

Mel hugged herself with her free hand, trying to control her trembling body.

'Mum, oh Mum. Help me, Mum,' she cried. But nobody heard her and eventually she was cried out. Despite the fact that it was starting to get light, her exhausted body needed to rest and she fell into a fitful sleep. She dreamt of the Bogey Man that her mother had warned her about when she was young, a man she'd thought was fictional, but now she knew that he really did exist.

*****

Big Ed was nowhere to be found. The closed sign hung from the front door and a number of punters had banged on it surprised to be confronted by police who either sent them away or brought them in for questioning. The word out that something was amiss and the shadier characters kept away from his shop. Claire and Ron had only spent a little time at his base before concluding that they wouldn't get any information from there.

194

'Where do we go next?' said Claire, asking herself as well as Ron.

'We need to find out about his associates and hope that one of them can lead us to him.'

'I know that, but how?'

Ron had no idea and was pondering their predicament.

'The party location. We need to go there. He might have taken her there,' said Claire.

'I don't think so. Would he be that stupid?'

'Do you have a better idea?' It was a fair point.

Ken was surprised to see them again and greeted them as if they were long lost relatives. This is all very well, thought Claire. They were in a rush but she tried not to show him, not wanting to hurt his feelings for some reason she couldn't fathom.

'Yes, nice to see you too, Ken,' she said.

Ron coughed.

'We need the address where you used to take the girls. It may help us to locate my sister.'

He explained that there had been two separate venues and he gave them both addresses. Ron knew the areas well from his taxi driving. They said their goodbyes once again and left in a hurry.

They were too late at the first place, it looked as if it had been gutted and all that was left was the shell of the house. They struck lucky at the second location.

Sandy was absolutely shattered. He'd sent her back to London the previous night and she'd already sorted the first house. Now she had to do this one and get back to feed the girl. She sighed, placing another heavy plastic bag in the corner of the big room with the two already there. The journey from city to city was only two hours, which was fine. But they were out in the sticks and by the time she hired a car and negotiated the windy roads it would be at least four hours from door to door, and that was only if everything went smoothly. It hadn't the first time and she tentatively placed a hand on her cheek and winced. It was still painful even though the beating had happened two days before and he wouldn't have done it if she'd followed his instructions. It had saved time but he wasn't happy that she'd used her own licence for the hire car, and hadn't bothered to obtain a stolen one like he'd told her to. He was under a lot of stress and she knew he couldn't help himself, but this was the worst beating he'd given her and Sandy was beginning to feel that it wasn't her fault this time. The woman on the train didn't believe her story that she'd drank too much and fallen over. She'd told her that she could leave and that there were organisations that would help her. Sandy took the card out of her pocket and studied it, wondering if it was possible to start over. Her ringing phone brought her back to the present and she sighed when she saw it was him. She hoped that she wasn't in trouble again.

Claire noticed that the woman's work rate increased once she'd hung up the phone, despite the fact that she was also crying and hastily wiping the tears from her face as she was going about her business. She finished loading the bags and dragged them one by one down the two flights of stairs, and out onto the main road. There was a skip at the end of the street and Claire and Ron watched as she struggled to lift each bag into it. She failed with the third and had a quick look around to ensure she wasn't being watched, before removing some of the bottles, old clothes and syringes and throwing them into the skip separately. Exhausted, she slowly climbed back up the stairs and looked around. It was all clear and Sandy went downstairs and satisfied herself that there was no incriminating evidence left in the house. She washed her hands and face, and dried them on the old towel in the bathroom.

She left the house, forgetting to remove the old towel, locked the front door and put the keys in her bag, planning to throw them out of the train window between stations. Wearily she made her way to the underground to start her journey northwards, hoping that his mood would improve by the time she got there.

The journey to Manchester was uneventful and Claire and Ron followed Sandy from the time she entered the underground station in London, until she arrived at the old rundown farmhouse out in the sticks. They didn't have an address but she would be able to give the twins the location of the nearest village and with Ron's help, clear directions from the village to the farmhouse.

They quickly entered the old farmhouse just to be sure and looked around. They eventually found the miserable room where Mel was being held prisoner. She was sleeping and as far as Claire could see, she wasn't physically damaged except for a few red marks on her neck and the pale and drawn appearance even in sleep, due to the worry of her current circumstances Claire assumed.

'It's going to be all right,' said Claire. 'We'll send someone to save you as soon as we can.'

Mel turned over in her sleep and smiled, muttering, *'Thank you,'* as she did so.

'She can hear me! I can talk to my new sister when she's sleeping, just like I did with the twins!'

'Calm down, Claire. It might only be coincidence and she's having a nice dream to escape from her current dire circumstances.'

But Claire knew she was right and wanted to get to her brothers as soon as possible so they could start the mission to save their sister.

*****

For some reason unclear to him, Carol had distanced herself even further from Graham. She hadn't exactly blamed him for Mel's abduction, but had said that if they'd been a *normal* family, Mel wouldn't have got into the taxi that night and therefore wouldn't have been abducted later on. When Graham had tried to explain that her logic was flawed they'd fallen out and she wouldn't let him anywhere near her house. The twins knew how distressed their father was and didn't want him to be on his own, so they'd insisted he move in with them until Mel was found safe and sound. They'd also taken time off work to concentrate all their efforts on finding their sister.

Graham hadn't slept for the two days since his daughter had been taken and Tony looked as his father's drawn, haggard face, and hair that seemed to be going greyer by the second.

'Here, Dad. Drink this.'

He took the mug of hot milk without a word and started sipping. 'What if he's hurt her? I couldn't bear to lose her as well.'

'It's not going to happen, Dad. I want you to go and lie down after you've drank that and we'll speak to the police in the meantime, to find out what progress they've made.'

Graham didn't want to sleep in case some news came in and he missed it.

'We'll wake you if there's any news, Dad. I can't imagine how you're feeling but you need to look after yourself so you can be there for Mel when they find her,' said Jim. They were all frightened about what could happen, but he was determined to try and stay positive for his father's sake.

'Here, this will help.' He handed his father a sleeping tablet and helped him up from the sofa as if he were an old man. Jim took his father's mug and escorted him to the bedroom. He watched him take the tablet and he closed the curtains. Graham lay on the bed.

198

'Don't leave me too long, son.'

'Of course not and I'll wake you if there's any news.'

He closed the door and returned to the lounge. Tony looked at his brother and the unanswered question hung in the air between them. Why hadn't Claire been in touch to help out?

*****

Satisfied with the progress made by Claire and Ron, Gabriella was able to concentrate on other matters within her area of responsibility. Ken was totally bored when she appeared unexpectedly with her customary whoosh. He could see from her expression that it was time for him to leave and he closed his eyes for a second, trying to sum up courage and not look frightened in front of his adored heroine. Feeling composed and slightly less stressed he looked at the angel.

'What do you want me to do?'

'I want you to prove me right, Kenneth and to live a good life.' She gave a special smile and if he could have granted her the universe he would have.

'I'll try not to let you down.'

'Say goodbye to Kenneth and close your eyes.'

'Where am I going?'

'All will become clear, Kenneth. Say goodbye.'

He did as he was bid. Kenneth saw a few stars on a black background, spinning around inside and outside his head, their number multiplied and he started to feel dizzy. The black background became smaller and smaller as the stars blurred and seemed to join together. All he could see wherever he looked was one intensely bright light, and he couldn't work out whether it was in his very being or in the outside world. He only knew that it was warm and seemed to be calling to him. He followed it and wasn't at all frightened.

She gave one final scream and the baby slithered out and was picked up by the midwife who wiped it and wrapped the crying infant in a baby blanket.

'Your son, Frau Mueller,' said the midwife in heavily accented English as she handed the baby to his mother. The mother looked at the perfect being in her arms, and felt a surge of love that surprised her with its intensity. She knew that she'd do anything for this boy and if anyone tried to harm him or make him unhappy, God help them. Her husband stroked her hair and she remembered that she wasn't alone. She kissed the baby's head and handed him to his father. She could tell from the expression on Otto's face that he felt exactly the same as she did, and her love for her husband grew even more.

Gabriella brushed her hands together at a job well done as she looked at the happy scene and smiled, satisfied that Kenneth would have the best chance she could give him to live a good life. The rest was now up to him.

*****

They arrived at the flat as her brothers were in the living room. There was a chat show on the TV, but both were lost in their own thoughts and neither appeared to be watching. They sat up straight at the same time. They know, thought Ron as Tony looked at Jim.

'She's here isn't she?'

His brother nodded and they waited for their sister to speak.

'I know where she is.'

'Is she okay?'

Claire told them that there was little physical harm but she couldn't say the same for their sister's mental state.

200

'She was sleeping. But she's fifteen years old and with a man who arranged for her friends to be raped. She's bound to be terrified about what's going to happen to her, especially if she knows he's the one who abducted her.'

Claire told them the location and Tony looked it up on his tablet. 'Even if we leave now, we won't get there for another four hours at the very least.'

'And the police said they're going to be interviewing the scum who went to that party, so the Big Ed tosser is bound to find out about that soon.'

'And when he does find out, if any of those know about the farmhouse, he'll want to move on quickly.'

The twins were doing their tag-team conversation and Ron was the only one who found it disconcerting. But he was also impressed with their deductions and told her so. He suggested that they contact the police and tell them the address.

'Are you still there, Claire?'

'Yes. You need to contact the police so they can arrange to get someone there, in case he moves and we lose him. Not sure how you're going to explain it though.'

Ron shook his head. For a bright girl she could be incredibly stupid at times.

'Anonymous email,' said the twins, and their sister shrugged to Ron, acknowledging that she'd had a blonde moment.

'Good idea. We're...'

Ron nudged her.

'I mean I'm going to go back to keep an eye on things and I'll try to let you know if anything changes before the police arrive.'

Jim woke his father and told him that the police had called and had received an anonymous tip-off while he'd been sleeping. Graham was still feeling groggy so got ready to leave the flat with his sons, not yet fully aware enough to ask any intelligent questions.

Tony logged on to his secret URL while they were in the car and sent an email to the address that had been given in the missing person news bulletin, shortly after Mel had been abducted. He was rather pleased with his own *Guardian Angel* email address.

*****

It wasn't going to plan and Big Ed was seething. Despite his earlier warning, Sandy had yet again failed to follow his instructions and he'd had to teach her another lesson. Already annoyed because he couldn't reach any of the party guys, he'd been heavy handed and she wouldn't be any use to him now other than fetching and carrying for the girl. It was different this time too. He rubbed his arm where she'd bitten it and although crying for him to stop, she'd had a defiant look about her. He'd have to bring her back into line when all this was over and he'd be glad when the girl was out of his hands. His thoughts wandered and he wondered whether to have a go at the girl himself, but soon put that out of his mind, knowing how much he'd earn for such a good looker who hadn't been touched. Money was always his overriding influence. He would get Sandy to confirm it, but he was almost sure the girl was a virgin by the way she acted. But first he'd need to find someone to take her off his hands. He logged on to his laptop and typed in the password for his database. Big Ed selected half a dozen names and started making the calls. By the time he'd made three, he suspected that all was not well and this was confirmed on the fourth call.

'Don't call here again, Ed,' Keith Layton sounded threatening and Ed wasn't happy.

'Remember who you're talking to, Keith. I don't take kindly...'

202

'Remember who I'm talking to? You're having a fucking laugh, mate. Because of you, Roger and the other two are already *helping the police with their enquiries*,' the sarcasm in his voice wasn't lost on Big Ed, 'and it's only a matter of time before they catch up with you. And you want to know whether I want the girl? What are you on? Piss off and don't bother me again if you know what's good for you.' He hung up before Big Ed could respond and Sandy heard his roar from the other end of the house.

'I'm coming, I'm coming,' she shouted. Her intention was to do things as slowly as possible, playing for time. Ironically, she didn't need to pretend. The pain was intense and she winced with every step she took, hoping that her message had got through and that they'd arrive before he whisked them away somewhere out of their reach. The realization hit her that she was his prisoner as much as the girl and she knew she had to get away from him, by whatever means necessary.

*****

Janet loved working for DI Sparks and his team, although at times the job could be very traumatic. She had a daughter the same age as the missing girl and her heart went out to the parents. Her job was to quickly scan the emails about the missing girl and to file them into three separate folders. Urgent, non-urgent and the slush pile. The public were wonderful but had their fair share of loonies and Janet had just finished reading about a UFO sighting, the sender informing the police that the abductors were from another planet. She'd been staring at the screen for three hours non-stop and her eyes were getting tired. Having asked for assistance she'd received the usual response that they'd do what they could but resources were tight and she'd have to manage on her own for now. The additional staff that the DCI had seconded to the unit were all out on the ground, gathering as much information as they could. She needed a drink and the bathroom so Janet took a break, used the facilities and got herself a coffee. The DI called her in and she told him about the hundred or so emails she hadn't yet filtered. Although he knew she needed a break he could make her feel guilty with a look and she returned to her desk, knackered but determined to crack on and hoping that the caffeine would soon kick-in.

About an hour later she read the email from Sandy. *Shes here and hes gonna sell her.* The address of the farmhouse appeared underneath. Janet quickly printed off the email. Seeing that DI Sparks was on the phone in his office with the door closed, she gave the piece of paper to DS James. She returned to her desk and a few minutes later shouted to anyone who would listen. The DI and DS appeared at her desk and she pointed out the *Guardian Angel* email, which contained the same address as the one she'd already given to them. All hell broke out in the section and Janet tried to contain her excitement. Hopefully they'd be able to catch this one and the girl would be rescued safe and sound.

*****

Jim parked the car where they could see the farmhouse, but hidden from those inside, and waited. They hadn't heard any sirens and there wasn't a police presence and they wondered what was going on. Graham was the first to voice his concerns.

'Where's the police?' He picked up his mobile phone as he spoke and searched for DI Sparks' number.

'What are you doing, Dad?' Jim asked, but Graham was already connected. Janet had answered in the absence of the detectives.

'I'm sorry, Mr Sylvester. There have been err... developments, which I'm not obliged to discuss at the moment. Suffice to say that the DCI or DI will be in touch as soon as they can.'

'This is my daughter we're talking about, and if there've been developments I need to know about them!' Graham screamed into the phone and Janet pulled her handset away from her ear.

'But, Mr Sylvester...' Janet thought of her own daughter again and changed her mind. She couldn't help herself. 'I shouldn't really tell you this but they're on their way to Manchester. They've had a tip off that they have to investigate and the force up there are getting a team ready to carry out the operation.'

'I'm already at the farmhouse in Manchester, Janet. How come I can get here...' Tony turned and grabbed the phone out of his father's hand.

'Err, Janet is it? Tell DI Sparks that we received an anonymous email giving us this address. We couldn't get hold of him so forwarded the email and made our way here. Thanks, love. Bye.' He killed the connection.

Jim gave his brother a warning look but said nothing.

'Right, what's going on? I'm not totally stupid.' Graham's emotions were all over the place and he didn't know how much more he could take.

'It's like I said to Janet, Dad. We received an email so we sent it to the police.' Tony spoke quietly and calmly, trying to pacify his anxious father and cool the atmosphere in the car, which felt like the minutes before a battle.

'But why didn't you tell me...'

'I did, when you woke up,' Jim interrupted. 'You must have still been half asleep and misheard me.'

Graham thought back to the flat and his son might have been right. He remembered Jim saying that the police had received a tip off, but once he'd been told that they'd found Mel everything else was a blur.

205

The twins tried to act relaxed while their father attempted to make sense of the situation.

'The main thing is that she's found. Let's go and get her.'

'Dad, they may be armed. I know it's hard, but we're going to have watch for the time being and wait for the police to arrive.'

'But what if...'

'If we hear anything or if they come outside before the police arrive, we'll do something.' Tony hoped it wouldn't come to that but the twins knew that Claire was in there and would let them know if Mel was in any immediate danger, or if they were getting ready to move.

Graham knew his sons were right but that didn't make him feel any better. He couldn't keep still and fidgeted, feeling like a trapped animal, ready to spring at the first opportunity.

He didn't have long to wait.

*****

She got to the room and was too slow to avoid his vicious slap, which knocked her to the ground.

'I'm sorry, I'm sorry,' she said, scurrying to the corner of the room. 'What do you want me to do, just tell me and I'll do it.' Sandy was absolutely terrified. In the past his rages had been cold, controlled and measured and he always seemed to know how much her body could take without putting her completely out of action or into hospital. She could see that this time, he was struggling to hold it together and she wasn't sure which side of him would win this particular fight.

Think, woman. Think, think, think. 'What do you want me to do? You know I love you. Shall I check on the girl...'

She knew she should be quiet but it was as if her terror had disconnected her brain and she had no control of the words coming out of her mouth.

'Shut up!' he took a step towards her. 'Just shut up.' Big Ed ran at Sandy and lifted his leg back to give her a kick. He stopped at the last moment, seeing the terror on her face. What was he doing?

Sandy cowered in the corner then squeezed her eyes shut, tensed her body and waited for the inevitable. When it didn't come, she risked a peep out of one eye. He was holding his head in his hands, taking big gulps of air and trying to get himself back in control. She got up very slowly and walked to his side. Tentatively, she put a hand on his shoulder and relaxed slightly when he didn't strike her or shout. He dropped his arms to his side, lifted his head and looked at her.

'Sorry about that,' he said as if the attack had been an accident. 'They're on to us and we need to move.'

'What do you want me to do?'

'Check that she's a virgin. She's no good to me if she isn't and if that's the case we get rid of her.'

'But, Ed...'

'Do you have a problem with that?' She noticed the monster beginning to raise its ugly head again.

'Of course not,' Sandy looked away, hoping he wouldn't see the lie. 'Can you give me ten minutes?' He looked confused so she elaborated. 'She might lie if I ask so I'm going to have to do a physical check.'

He agreed. 'Be as quick as you can. I'll get rid of everything and get a bag together.'

They walked to the room in silence.

'I'll be back in ten minutes. Make sure you're ready,' was his parting shot and Sandy was disappointed when he locked the door after she entered, her chances of releasing the girl and making a run for it now non-existent.

Mel was shocked that the woman's face was visible and also at the state of it. She took in the black eye, bent nose and bruises before standing up and facing the wall, and then the penny dropped. She'd seen enough movies to know that now she'd seen both their faces, it meant that they didn't care whether she recognized them, as she wouldn't be around to tell anyone. They were going to kill her. She tried her best to control her sobs but the thought of her immediate future terrified her.

'Turn around and sit down.' Sandy tried smiling at the youngster to calm her a little. 'We don't have much time so I want you to concentrate on what I'm saying.' No response and the girl wouldn't look at her. She went to put her hand on Mel's face to lift her head, but the girl shrank back. Sandy totally knew how she felt.

'Please. I want to help you so you're going to have to trust me.'

No response.

'We share the same enemy.' This last in a whisper and Mel lifted her eyes slowly and looked at her captor's face properly, for the first time. She saw her own fear mirrored in Sandy's eyes and it gave her a smidgen of hope.

Now that she had the girl's attention Sandy continued in hushed whispers. 'I'm supposed to physically check that you're a virgin, then we're supposed to be leaving here and...' she stopped suddenly. She didn't need to frighten the girl any further so changed tack. 'Anyway, that's not important. But this is, so you need to listen carefully, understand?'

'Do you understand me?' This she said with more urgency and Mel nodded.

'If he asks you say that you're a virgin okay?'

'But I am.' She'd hardly spoken since her abduction and her voice sounded strange to herself and hoarse to Sandy.

'Good and you can say that I stripped you and checked. This is very important or we'll both be in deep trouble.'

Mel nodded in understanding and Sandy continued. 'Now I'm going to unchain you and mess your clothes up a bit so you look as if you've re-dressed in a hurry. Don't try to make a run for it because he's locked us in, and don't fight me because I really am on your side. I've sent a message to the police and they should be here at any time now, so we'll just have to stall him as best we can.'

Mel nodded again, her mind working overtime trying to consider her options. She knew the woman was frightened and surely there'd be a better chance of escape if it was two against one, rather than just her trying to get away from both of them.

'I'll do whatever you tell me.'

'Good. And don't look at him or annoy him.' Yet again she nodded and Sandy unchained her and tied her hands loosely behind her back with an old rag. They heard the key in the door and she quickly undid a few buttons on Mel's blouse and pulled it out of her skirt. Mel already looked dishevelled from her time in captivity so Big Ed didn't notice any difference when he walked into the room.

'Let's go.'

'Of course, but, umm, we both need the loo. What do you want us to do?'

'Take her to the one downstairs and untie her to make it quicker. I'll be watching though so no funny business,' he addressed the last to Mel and she nodded without making eye contact.

*****

The twins had only been waiting a few minutes when they heard their sister's voice.

'They're getting ready to leave.'

Unable to respond due to their father's presence, Tony spoke first. 'Did you see that?'

'What,' said Graham, 'see what?'

'The front door opened a bit, then closed. What if they're leaving before the police arrive?'

Graham hadn't seen a thing but trusted the judgement of his sons. Sitting inactive in the car was driving him nuts and he wanted to get his daughter out of there, with or without the police. Not listening to his sub-conscious voice of reason he made a decision.

'Come on, let's go.'

Before they had a chance to move the front door opened. A big man walked out carrying two large bags. He opened the boot and made light work of throwing them in. His strength was obvious to the three men and each knew they wouldn't be able to take him on their own. The man opened the car front door and got into the driving seat.

'What now?'

'We wait,' Jim told his father. 'We have no choice.'

Five and then ten minutes passed. Even from their distance they heard the man shout and he left the car, slamming the door behind him.

'I don't like the look of this,' said Tony getting out of the car. The big man was angry and they all left the car as quickly as they could and ran to the house, concern for Mel at the forefront and caution thrown to the wind.

*****

She did actually need to use the toilet. She remembered from a very young age how her mother used to laugh at her shyness, or try to cajole her, but had always ended up giving in and leaving her alone. Mel had never been able to perform with an audience and she experienced the same problem now, only it was multiplied tenfold by terror at her circumstances.

210

'Come on, Mel love.' It was the first time that Sandy had used her name and Mel hoped this was a good sign.

'I can't go if someone's watching. Sorry.'

'He'll go berserk if I leave you alone, you've got to go.'

'But you don't understand. I just can't.' Mel was desperate now trying even harder, but it was impossible with the stress of knowing they would both be hurt if she wasn't quick.

'I'll have to leave it.'

Sandy nodded, knowing that Ed was probably at the limit of his patience. The door opened and she was proved right.

'Hurry up,' he growled at both of them and Sandy's eyes pleaded with Mel.

'I'm sorry.' She started to shake as he approached.

Sandy stood in front of Mel and closed her eyes. 'Please, give us just a minute and wait outside. Please, Ed. It'll be quicker and we...' She knew her pleading wasn't working but if she moved, he'd go straight for the girl. She didn't budge, the last vestige of personality and stubbornness rooting her legs to the spot. He hesitated for a moment, briefly wondering if she hadn't sensed his mood or if she were totally stupid. Mel pulled her underwear up as quickly as she could, trying to make herself invisible at the same time. Her movements weren't quick enough and Sandy crashed into her with the force from his punch. Mel fell to the floor. Sandy's head glanced off the side of the bowl and she also landed on the floor. Big Ed smiled to himself and moved nearer the toilet, but turned abruptly when he heard a warlike roar. Years of street fighting had honed his instincts and he quickly assessed that the older man was weaker, and out of control. It took one quick heavy punch to put Graham out of action and he lay on the floor semi-conscious.

Big Ed had temporarily forgotten about the girl when he was dealing with his attacker. Thinking quickly, Mel had crawled towards the two men who'd entered the room with her father, hoping that they were here to save her and not yet registering why they looked strangely familiar. The twins started to approach her captor cautiously. Big Ed judged that he could take them on individually, but would struggle to overcome both at the same time. The glint of silver stopped them in their tracks. Mel was now behind them so he would have to fight off the twins before being able to get to her. They were at an impasse, but the twins were happy that their sister was out of immediate danger.

Not taking his eyes off the big man, Tony put a hand behind his back and tapped his sister's shoulder.

'Stay behind us whatever happens.' She couldn't reach the door without risk so was more than happy to follow his advice.

Graham started to groan and Big Ed knew that he wouldn't be able to contain the situation for much longer. He backed further into the room towards Sandy. Grabbing her as if she were a rag doll, he lifted her and put her body in front of his, using her as a shield. He placed his forearm around her neck and squeezed to show her he meant business. Sandy felt like her eyes would pop out of her head as she wondered what he planned to do next. His knife hand was next to her throat and the onlookers knew he wouldn't hesitate to use it. Neither twin was confident of tackling him without harm coming to the woman and Big Ed slowly made his way to the door, back first, so he could keep his eyes on all of them. Closing the door behind him with his foot, he threw Sandy to the floor, retrieved the padlock from his pocket and locked it.

Mel got up from the floor and ran to her father. Graham was bruised and sore but forgot about his aches and pains as he held his beloved daughter in his arms, both crying and laughing at the same time.

'Mel, these are your brothers.'

'Nice to meet you, Mel,' said Tony and he winked at his sister. 'We'll say hello properly once we've got us out of here.' And he carried on kicking the door with his brother. Mel took a second to look at her brothers - they were well cool. Her friends were going to drool over these two and she was going to have some fun showing them off. Thinking of her friends made her realize that she may not have seen them again, and what about her mother? Delayed shock set-in and Graham held his daughter's trembling body while her brothers worked on the door. It took a few minutes before the wooden door shattered and the twins climbed through it and ran outside. It was as they suspected. The car, the man and woman had long gone. They could make out a black van and a number of cars in the distance heading toward the farmhouse and as the vehicles neared, Jim rightly assumed that the police had arrived at long last.

Supporting his fragile daughter Graham joined the twins and one glance told the police that the girl wasn't in any trouble. Mel had had enough drama to last her a lifetime.

'They're my father and brothers,' she called as loudly as she could in case there was any doubt.

The police secured the area within minutes and the twins quickly briefed them on the turn of events. As a jacket was put around Mel who was still shivering, she looked at the officer and then her father.

'I want my Mum.'

Carol answered on the second ring. 'She's safe,' was all he said before handing the phone to his daughter.

213

They hung up a little later, with Graham promising to get Mel home as soon as he could.

Carol couldn't stop crying. She looked heavenward and thanked the Gods of all religions she could think of. Then she said thanks to Jesus, Buddha and Mohammed. Believing she'd covered all bases regarding religion she now concentrated on those still living and thanked the police and her estranged partner, but mostly she thanked Graham's sons for wanting to help their sister, even though she hadn't wanted to know them and she had shown nothing but indifference toward their existence. She checked Mel's room which was in pristine condition. She'd tidied and cleaned it during the night hours when she couldn't sleep for worry about what was happening to her daughter. Finally, she went to the kitchen to prepare all of Mel's favourite dishes. Her daughter would know how much she was loved and how her mother had missed her. Carol never wanted to let her out of her sight again, ever.

The police agreed that further interviews could take place in London and made arrangements for a car to escort them on their return journey back to their home city. The twins made their way back to Jim's car, telling their father and new sister that they'd see them there.

'That went rather well,' said Claire surprising her brothers who hadn't sensed her presence, due to the stress of the rescue. 'Well done.'

'Thanks, Claire. Couldn't have done it without you.'

'You speak to your sister?' came their father's voice.

The twins hadn't noticed that he and Mel had caught up and were directly behind them. There was no way to deny it so the brothers stopped walking and turned to their father, both nodding as they did so.

'I don't believe in all that stuff myself but I suppose we're all different, and if it works for you...' He shrugged and left the rest of the sentence unfinished.

'I was so sorry to hear about your sister,' said Mel, keen to say the right thing and make a good impression.

'After all she's been through, how thoughtful,' said Claire. 'I'm off, see you later.' She laughed as her brothers tried their hardest to ignore her. They didn't need to for much longer as they sensed when she'd left.

Chapter 15

Sandy slipped in and out of consciousness until the pain of being slapped on the face brought her fully back to her senses. Still dazed, she attempted to lift a hand to rub her cheek then realized her hands were tied tightly together behind her back. She was incredibly thirsty but the gag wouldn't allow her to lick her dry lips. She didn't know where they were, except that they were in the middle of nowhere and he had a vicious and determined look in his eyes. She shook her head and he must have seen the fear in her eyes as he gave a satisfied smile. Sandy closed her eyes again and attempted to control her breathing, she wasn't finished yet and her brain searched for possible ways of escape. She tried coughing and pretending to choke but he sat calmly until she stopped. That's when she realized that he held her responsible for the girl's freedom, and he intended to make her pay.

He got out of the car, walked round the front to the passenger's side, and opened the door leisurely, whistling to himself as if he were on a happy day out with his lover.

'Come on then, out you get.' He grabbed her arm roughly and flung her to the floor.

'What shall we do with you then?' Sandy rolled herself into a ball and closed her eyes hoping that it would be over quickly. That was no fun for Big Ed. He kicked her knees, forcing her to straighten them and told her to look at him. When she refused to open her eyes, he shouted. 'OPEN, YOUR, EYES!' Each word emphasized and accompanied by a kick.

Resigned to a painful end whether or not she did as he ordered, Sandy refused to open her eyes and this drove him apoplectic. He shouted and screamed with each blow or kick and she cried out in pure agony, still refusing to open her eyes. He stopped eventually and used his hands to force them open. Seeing only the whites drove him to distraction and Sandy's last thought was one of satisfaction before she finally slipped into welcome unconsciousness.

The pain had been agonising, but suddenly it stopped. Sandy had the sensation of hands pulling at her but that stopped too. She felt herself floating, wondering for a second where she was. Then she realised that she didn't care because the pain had gone, along with Big Ed and she knew she wouldn't have to suffer another beating from him, ever again.

*****

Claire was so proud of her brothers and father and her soul swelled with love for them and her new sister. She knew that it would take ages for Mel to get over her ordeal and that it would scar her for life. But Mel and the twins would benefit from knowing each other and Claire was so pleased that she was safe. She was looking forward to seeing how their relationship developed in the future.

'Let's go and see Gabriella,' said Ron, and Claire was happy to do so, having said goodbye to the twins.

'I thought because I speak to my brothers, that I would be able to progress and speak to my parents and maybe Jay. Although Gabriella told me the contact with my mother was a one off I didn't want to believe her.'

Ron nodded. 'But you know now don't you?'

'I wasn't sure.'

'Claire, what you and your brothers have is some sort of natural and special gift. Be grateful for it. It's extremely rare.'

'How do you know all this?'

'I have other talents,' he said mysteriously and left her wondering what they were. He looked away so that she wouldn't see the twinkle in his eyes. She didn't even realize she was special and he envied her. It was wrong, he knew and sometimes teasing her a little made him feel better.

They were surprised to see that Gabriella was already waiting for them and she was pleased when they told her how Mel had been saved.

'You both did very well but it's a shame the perpetrator escaped.'

'I thought that you would send someone to look after that side of things?' said Claire and Gabriella explained that she'd had to take two of her assistants to deal with a crisis in Africa.

'Nothing to do with your mother and her friend,' she explained, knowing exactly how Claire's mind worked.

'And now I have some news.' She looked at them both for a while and Claire felt as if she were at a job interview. Ron's demeanour was far more relaxed. Knowing that Gabriella did everything in her own time, by her rules, he waited patiently for her to continue. They both sensed the subtle change in the atmosphere and Claire knew her news would determine the location of her future.

'Claire. By now you must realise that you have special talents that are few and far between?'

'Yes.' It was a whisper. *Please don't send me to hell, please don't send me to hell.*

'The Committee have made a decision about your future.'

Claire closed her eyes. *Here it comes.*

'And, Ron...' she smiled at him but Claire interrupted.

'Err Gabriella, we all know where Ron's going to end up, I thought this was about my future?'

'And that reaction is precisely why I can't leave you alone with your talents,' she shushed Claire when she went to interrupt again. 'Talented, kind and thoughtful, yes. But you are also impatient, impulsive and foolhardy at times, Claire...'

'But...'

'Shall I come back later?' That did the trick.

'You know that we face a constant battle against evil? From the evil souls on Earth and those feeble individuals who allow themselves to be led by them. Also from those sent by the master of evil himself. You must have realised by now that we need all the help we can get?'

She signalled that Ron and Claire could ask questions this time but for once, Claire had nothing to say.

'Well, the Committee want your help, Claire. You are getting stronger all the time and they want you to stay here and to help fight some of that evil by using the natural talents you have.'

'Does that mean I'm not going to hell?'

'You were never going there, young lady.' Claire couldn't understand why Gabriella and Ron found this so funny, and she joined in with their laughter not really knowing why.

Gabriella stopped eventually and turned serious again. 'If you're not interested we'll send you on your merry way. What do you think?'

'What about Ron?'

'Ah. Now we come to Ron. They've given you a choice,' she pointed a long finger at him. 'If Claire agrees to do this...' Gabriella knew Claire's mind before she did, and already knew that she would agree, 'then you decide whether you want to partner her, or move on to heaven and rest forever in eternity.'

Ron was undecided. 'So, if I go to heaven then change my mind, what happens?'

'Some, like myself, are taken from heaven and put to work, Ron. But the choice isn't ours.'

He looked at Claire and wondered if she could manage without him.

'If you decide to move on, I have someone else lined up to help Claire. She redeemed herself before her painful death, and is on her way now, though she still has many lessons to learn.'

'So my choice is stay here and try to keep Claire out of trouble? And I'll still be able to visit my family occasionally?' Gabriella nodded.

'Or my soul rests in peace for eternity and there are wonders and miracles there beyond my imagination?'

'Got it. And while you're making up your mind, Ron. I want you, Claire, to go and see how your brothers and sister are getting along.'

'But if Ron decides to go to heaven, he won't be here when I return.'

'Correct. That's the way it goes, Claire.'

'But it'll be like losing one of my family, all over again.' Ron had become a substitute father figure and she realised she was very fond of him. Claire was devastated that he might not be there on her return and was reluctant to leave. Ron took her hand and pulled her into an embrace.

'Everything will be all right. Don't worry.' He stroked her hair like he used to with Libby when she was upset.

'So you're staying?'

'I didn't say that. Now do what Gabriella says. Go on, there's a good girl.'

Claire reluctantly broke the embrace. Tears in her eyes she floated away, not knowing who or what would be there when she eventually returned.

Acknowledgements

Thanks to my husband Allan for listening (or doing a good job of pretending to listen), to my fabulous editor Jill Turner and wonderful cover designer Jessica Bell. Thanks also to all my friends for their support.

Author's Note

Thank you for purchasing this book. I hope you enjoyed reading it as much as I did writing it.

If you like what you've read so far, you may be interested in my other books:

Beyond Life (The Afterlife Series Book 2)
Beyond Destiny (The Afterlife Series Book 3)
Beyond Possession (The Afterlife Series Book 4)
Beyond Limits (The Afterlife Series Book 5)

Unlikely Soldiers Book 1 (Civvy to Squaddie)
Unlikely Soldiers Book 2 (Secrets & Lies)
Unlikely Soldiers Book 3 (Friends & Revenge)
Unlikely Soldiers Book 4 (Murder & Mayhem)

The Island Dog Squad Book 1 (Sandy's Story)
- FREE AT THIS LINK
https://dl.bookfunnel.com/wdh6nl8p08

The Island Dog Squad Book 2 (Another Crazy Mission)
The Island Dog Squad Book 3 (People Problems)

Court Out (A Netball Girls' Drama)

Non-fiction:

Zak, My Boy Wonder

And for children:

Reindeer Dreams
Jason the Penguin (He's Different)
Jason the Penguin (He Learns to Swim)

Further information is on my website https://debmcewansbooksandblogs.com or you can connect with me on Facebook: https://www.facebook.com/DebMcEwansbooksandblogs/?ref=bookmarks

About the Author

Following a career of over thirty years in the British Army, I moved to Cyprus with my husband to become weather refugees.

I've written children's books about Jason the penguin and Barry the reindeer, and books for a more mature audience about dogs, the afterlife, soldiers and netball players, along with a non-fiction book about a very special boy named Zak.

'Court Out (A Netball Girls' Drama)' is a standalone novel. Using netball as an escape from her miserable home life, Marsha Lawson is desperate to keep the past buried and to forge a brighter future. But she's not the only one with secrets. When two players want revenge, a tsunami of emotions is released at a tournament, leaving destruction in its wake. As the wave starts spreading throughout the team, can Marsha and the others escape its deadly grasp, or will their emotional baggage pull them under, with devastating consequences for their families and team-mates?

The Afterlife series was inspired by ants. I was in the garden contemplating whether to squash an irritating ant or to let it live. I wondered whether anyone *up there* decides the same about us and thus the series was born. Book six is currently in the planning stage and I'm not yet sure when the series will end.

'The Island Dog Squad' is a series of novellas told from a dog's point of view. It was inspired by the rescue dog we adopted in 2018. The real Sandy is a sensitive soul, not quite like her fictional namesake, and the other characters are based on Sandy's real-life mates.

'Zak, My Boy Wonder', is a non-fiction book co-written with Zak's Mum, Joanne Lythgoe. I met Jo and her children when we moved to Cyprus in 2013. Jo shared her story over a drink one night and I was astounded, finding it hard to believe that a family could be treated with such cruelty, indifference and a complete lack of compassion and empathy. This sounded like a tale from Victorian times and not the twenty-first century. When I suggested she share her story, Jo said she was too busy looking after both children – especially Zak who still needed a number of surgeries – and didn't have the emotional or physical energy required to dig up the past. Almost fourteen years after Zak's birth, Jo felt ready to share this harrowing but inspirational tale of a woman and her family who refused to give up and were determined not to let the judgemental, nasty, small-minded people grind them down.

When I'm not writing I love spending time with Allan and our rescue dog Sandy. I also enjoy keeping fit and socialising, and will do anything to avoid housework.